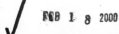

The Story of Ernestine

Texts and Translations

Chair: Robert J. Rodini
Series editors: Jane K. Brown, Edward M. Gunn, Michael R. Katz,
Carol S. Maier, Kathleen Ross, and English Showalter

The Texts and Translations series was founded in 1991 to provide students and teachers with important texts not readily available or not available at an affordable price and in high-quality translations. The books in the series are intended for students in upper-level undergraduate and graduate courses in national literatures in languages other than English, comparative literature, ethnic studies, area studies, translation studies, women's studies, and gender studies. The Texts and Translations series is overseen by an editorial board composed of specialists in several national literatures and in translation studies.

Texts

1. Isabelle de Charrière. *Lettres de Mistriss Henley publiées par son amie.* Ed. Joan Hinde Stewart and Philip Stewart. 1993.
2. Françoise de Graffigny. *Lettres d'une Péruvienne.* Introd. Joan DeJean and Nancy K. Miller. 1993.
3. Claire de Duras. *Ourika.* Ed. Joan DeJean. Introd. Joan DeJean and Margaret Waller. 1994.
4. Eleonore Thon. *Adelheit von Rastenberg.* Ed. and introd. Karin A. Wurst. 1996.
5. Emilia Pardo Bazán. *"El encaje roto" y otros cuentos.* Ed. and introd. Joyce Tolliver. 1996.
6. Marie Riccoboni. *Histoire d'Ernestine.* Ed. Joan Hinde Stewart and Philip Stewart. 1998.

Translations

1. Isabelle de Charrière. *Letters of Mistress Henley Published by Her Friend.* Trans. Philip Stewart and Jean Vaché. 1993.
2. Françoise de Graffigny. *Letters from a Peruvian Woman.* Trans. David Kornacker. 1993.
3. Claire de Duras. *Ourika.* Trans. John Fowles. 1994.
4. Eleonore Thon. *Adelheit von Rastenberg.* Trans. George F. Peters. 1996.
5. Emilia Pardo Bazán. *"Torn Lace" and Other Stories.* Trans. María Cristina Urruela. 1996.
6. Marie Riccoboni. *The Story of Ernestine.* Trans. Joan Hinde Stewart and Philip Stewart. 1998.

MARIE RICCOBONI

The Story of Ernestine

Edited and translated by
Joan Hinde Stewart
and Philip Stewart

The Modern Language Association of America
New York   1998

©1998 by The Modern Language Association of America
All rights reserved. Printed in the United States of America

For information about obtaining permission to reprint material from
MLA book publications, send your request by mail (see address below),
e-mail (permissions@mla.org), or fax (212 477-9863).

Library of Congress Cataloging-in-Publication Data

Riccoboni, Marie Jeanne de Heurles Laboras de Mezières, 1713–1792.
[Histoire d'Ernestine. English]
The story of Ernestine / Marie Riccoboni ; edited and translated
by Joan Hinde Stewart and Philip Stewart.
p.   cm. — (Texts and translations. Translations ; 7)
Includes bibliographical references.
ISBN 0-87352-786-0 (paper)
I. Stewart, Joan Hinde. II. Stewart, Philip. III. Title. IV. Series.
PQ2027.R3H5513   1998
843' .5—dc21   98-38996

ISSN 1079-2538

Cover illustration: *Portrait of a Young Woman*, by
Marie-Louise-Elisabeth Vigée-Lebrun (1755–1842). Oil on canvas.
Robert Dawson Evans Collection. Courtesy of Museum of Fine Arts, Boston.

Printed on recycled paper

Published by The Modern Language Association of America
10 Astor Place, New York, New York 10003-6981

TABLE OF CONTENTS

INTRODUCTION

Histoire d'Ernestine was published in 1765 as the main new attraction in a collection of otherwise reissued short pieces including Marie Riccoboni's well-known sequel to *La vie de Marianne*, by Pierre Marivaux. Riccoboni had already established considerable appeal with the reading public through her first three novels, published in the space of just a couple of years. *Lettres de Mistriss Fanni Butlerd* (1757), a spare work of autobiographical inspiration, analyzes a love affair from beginning to end. *Histoire de M. le marquis de Cressy* (1758), about an ambitious man who drives one woman to a nunnery and another to suicide, revolted and fascinated readers. *Lettres de Mylady Juliette Catesby* (1759), which was to join Jean Jacques Rousseau's *Julie ou la nouvelle Héloïse* (1761) as the two most frequently published novels of the eighteenth century, is the story of a spirited woman who, angry at first over her lover's fickleness, eventually forgives and marries him.

After these initial successes, Riccoboni had gone on to write *Amélie* (1762), freely adapted from Henry Fielding's *Amelia*, and *Histoire de Miss Jenny* (1764), which contained one of her few complicated plots. *The Story of Ernestine*, which came next, was to be followed by three more novels: *Lettres d'Adélaïde de Dammartin, comtesse de Sancerre*

(1767), *Lettres d'Elisabeth Sophie de Vallière* (1772), and *Lettres de Mylord Rivers* (1777), as well as original short stories and translations of several English plays.

Even independent of the critical and popular acclaim that was to greet *Ernestine,* the period of its publication was an exceptionally good one for Madame Riccoboni, as she was then signing her novels—or Marie Riccoboni, as she often signed her letters. Her full maiden name was Marie Jeanne de Heurles de Laboras, and she had also adopted the name Mézières (with various spellings) when she became an actress. The proceeds from her first novels permitted her to retire from the Comédie Italienne in 1761, putting an end to an acting career that dated back to 1734, and to devote herself to the writing career she had begun at age forty-three. In 1765 she turned fifty-two and, having separated years earlier from her actor-husband, Antoine François Riccoboni, was living with a devoted and self-effacing friend, Thérèse Biancolelli, a retired actress like herself.

By 1765 Marie Riccoboni was also enjoying the company of two Britons on extended visits to the Continent. One was the manager of London's Drury Lane Theatre, the most famous English actor of the century, David Garrick, who was in Paris with his wife. The other was a young Scot, Robert Liston, who had come to Paris in the summer of 1764 as tutor to the sons of the British diplomat Gilbert Elliot. David Hume, a Scottish philosopher and historian on the staff of the British embassy in Paris, brought Liston, destined to become a distinguished diplomat himself, to meet Riccoboni. Liston was soon a regular visitor in the modest flat she shared in the rue Poissonnière, and he began giving English lessons to her and Biancolelli. He was twenty-nine years Riccoboni's junior. Garrick left Paris in the spring of 1765 and Liston in 1766; she was to correspond with both for many years.

With Garrick she shared a deep interest in theater and maintained a warm professional friendship; he would send her books and plays to read and translate, keep her abreast of English literary trends, and mediate with the London publisher of her novels, with whom she had endless financial difficulties. With Liston, however, the situation was more complex, for she had fallen in love with him during those English lessons, and despite her awareness of the futility of an attachment so essentially one-sided, and so geographically and culturally, not to add chronologically, imbalanced, the intensity of her feelings never abated. Riccoboni had had lovers, but her astonishing passion for the young Scot was her most preoccupying and enduring one. For twenty years, as he pursued his peripatetic career and occasionally visited her in Paris, she wrote him beautiful and tender letters, often maternal, sometimes impassioned. Her last extant letter, dated September 1783—a little more than nine years before she died 7 December 1792, at seventy-nine—was to him. "Adieu," she concluded. "It is hard for me to leave you. This is madness, is it not?" (Nicholls 440).[1]

The novels before 1765 revolve mostly around the perfidy—or, at best (as in *Lettres de Mylady Juliette Catesby*), the weakness—of men. This theme finds its culmination with the 1764 publication of *Histoire de Miss Jenny*, as bleak a story, and with as thoroughgoing a male villain, as Riccoboni ever conceived. With *Ernestine*, in contrast, she produced a finely detailed portrait of triumphant first love, where the struggle is not against male villainy but against social and personal prejudice and ambition. The three novels that followed, although shaped differently, were also to end happily.

But even while *Ernestine* inaugurates a new mode for Riccoboni, it stands as much apart from her subsequently published novels as it does from those that precede it. For its concision and polish, for the exemplary honesty of its protagonists, for the shining, uncalculating intelligence of its heroine, *Ernestine* is essentially without parallel in Riccoboni's oeuvre. Whereas several of her novels (e.g., *Lettres de Mistriss Fanni Butlerd* and *Lettres de Mylady Juliette Catesby*) are set in the vague England of convention, which was the literary fashion in France, *Ernestine* is anchored in places familiar to a French reader: Paris (specifically the Faubourg Saint-Antoine) and its environs, including Montmartre. The story of the German-born heroine who must acquire a new language and a new set of values and who must even learn how to dress and use makeup may perhaps be read, at one level, as a story of successful cross-cultural relations.

But for all its apparent simplicity, this novel is about sexual enlightenment and social prejudice. It turns on an issue that much exercised the literary imagination of the eighteenth century: seduction, in all its links to money, reputation, and marriageability. In fact, in many ways *Ernestine* is a typical period romance: a nubile orphan, a handsome marquis, spontaneous love, virginity nonetheless preserved, obstacles overcome, finally marriage. This story may seem rather distant from us today; its leading characters are a moneyed aristocrat who at twenty-six thinks of his servants patronizingly as "my dear children" and a lovely girl who must manage not only to keep her chastity but also to avoid any appearance to the contrary. Yet the novel is more than an appealing period piece, thanks to the grace of Riccoboni's writing, her gently insistent feminism, and the generosity of a resolution in which nobility proves to be as much a matter of mind and heart as birth. This is a book about happiness and coming of age, and about the interplay of prudence and courage.

Riccoboni's story of a young woman of obscure birth who must make her way in the world has been compared with Samuel Richardson's *Pamela* (1740), but Ernestine is incapable of Pamela's subtle calculation, and her adventure covers only a fraction of the length of Pamela's. In fact, Riccoboni was an adept reader of English literature and tried her hand more than once at translation, while her own novels were being translated into English (by, among others, the novelist Frances Brooke). Riccoboni's originality is apparent when she is read against two contemporaries working in French who rank among the most compelling writers of the era: Isabelle de Charrière, Dutch by birth and Swiss by marriage, and Françoise de Graffigny, author of the very popular novel *Lettres d'une Péruvienne* (1747). Much of the feminist impact of the novels of Graffigny and Charrière has to do with the authors' refusal of traditional endings: Zilia, the Peruvian, has a fine opportunity to marry yet declines to do so, much to the disappointment of Graffigny's readers; and the heroines of Charrière's *Lettres neuchâteloises* (1784), *Lettres de Mistriss Henley publiées par son amie* (1784), and *Lettres écrites de Lausanne* (1785) know no clear ending at all. Mistress Henley, for example, for a host of seemingly minor reasons, is deeply unhappy with her rigidly rational husband; but in her last letter she confides that she doesn't know what will become of her, and we never learn whether she lives or dies.

Riccoboni, in contrast, wraps everything up neatly at the end. On the way, she steers a middle course between the extravagant plot of *Lettres d'une Péruvienne* (exoticism, war, kidnapping, accidents at sea, fabulous wealth) and the understatement of Charrière's first few novels, where nothing ever really seems to happen more eventful than the removal of a portrait from a wall or the disappearance of an Angora cat.

Riccoboni's feminism is more explicit. At the same time, her writing displays an exemplary sobriety and discretion. Take, for example, the scene of the initial encounter between the marquis de Clémengis and Ernestine. An apprentice miniature painter, the sixteen-year-old girl is putting the finishing touches on a portrait begun by her master, when the elegant aristocrat she recognizes as its model enters the studio. She says not a word but gestures to him to be seated and goes on working, looking back and forth between him and the likeness. The unexpectedness of such lack of ceremony thrills the world-weary marquis, who is stirred by her unaffected application to her work; her manner, which is neither deferential nor brazenly self-assured; her intuitive grasp of the uses of silence: "[T]his was a sort of adventure, simple but agreeable." The whole of Ernestine's brief story, for its understated elegance, for the resonant silences of incident and plot, may be similarly described.

Ernestine is a novel where feelings, events, and background are imparted by intimation. When we learn that certain women are "of less than the most scrupulous conduct," we are supposed to understand their moral laxness. Similarly, the stylized physical description characteristic of the period's novels belies, in Riccoboni's case, the richness of psychological detail: while the marquis's good looks are conveyed by no more than a brief allusion to his "distinguished attire and demeanor," we appreciate his appeal when we learn that an unnamed lady is impatiently awaiting his portrait. Even the isolating effect of accumulated deaths on the heroine is more implied than overtly stated. Riccoboni spends as few words on the disappearance of those who die as she does on description: the end comes quickly, without fuss. In the space of a few years and a few pages, Ernestine successively loses her natural, legal, and professional protectors: her young mother dies suddenly of no discernible cause; her adoptive mother falls ill a few years later and is gone within five days; her host and master succumbs a few years further on. Each time, we are made to understand, with a few phrases, the depth of her steadily maturing grief and to feel as well the void and the silence these absences create around her. The silence, about society's protocols and requirements, will be broken eventually, but almost too late, by her friend Henriette. Meanwhile, the situation obliges Ernestine to marshal not only her energy but also her artistic gifts.

For Ernestine, like her embroidering mother but unlike most protagonists in earlier sentimental novels, has to work, albeit in a distinguished trade. In this she resembles the author herself, who first acted and later wrote and translated for a living. Riccoboni was no leisured aristocrat; like Graffigny and Charrière, she was among the first women to support themselves through their writing. In *Ernestine*, she gives us a protagonist who learns to paint not for the drawing room but for the studio, one whose talent is no mere refinement but a survival skill. When Ernestine meets Clémengis, she is, and for a brief period remains—like her creator—a successful young working woman, and her studious application to her craft is partly responsible for the attraction she exerts. In this sense, she is exceptionally modern. She is dependent but not totally without resources, and as she matures, her ability to practice a trade is matched by her sturdy intuitions.

That is to say, Ernestine is neither the passive nor the victimized heroine found in numerous other novels of the period. She manages to negotiate questions of honor and appearances and to balance the precariousness of her social and economic situation against the potentially compromising nature of male generosity. And she finds happiness in the end, not because she is quietly won by the man she loves, and not really even because his influential relative has a change of heart, but because she deploys the energy of speech and action that alone can win both of them over. "Would I were dead!" she cries upon learning of Clémengis's misfortunes. "[O]h, why am I not dead, rather than learn that Monsieur de Clémengis is unhappy!" Taking bold action at the critical moment, courting society's derision for the sake of what she believes in, Ernestine claims him as her own. The docility and self-abnegation she displays early in the novel later give way to her private notions of justice and generosity: first she offers herself as a sacrifice to the marquis's desires, if that is what is required to "save" him, and at the end she rushes to his side as if to offer herself in marriage, even though he hasn't asked. Her idea of the *bienséances* ("propriety"), as one recent critic notes, would have shocked the classics (Kibédi Varga 982).

That serviceable vision of the good and the proper is consonant with Ernestine's respect for her own sexuality, and in this too she is distinct from other sentimental heroines. While she resists seduction, she hardly denies desire, and very nearly confesses to it, groping to come to terms with her feelings and expressing at the presence of Clémengis "I know not what delightful sentiment." As she admits later to Clémengis himself, "It is not you, Monsieur, it is myself that I fear." When she offers to submit to him, her motivations encompass both gratitude and desire.

A long central episode foregrounds the question of the heroine's virginity. When Henriette Duménil has finally been persuaded of what the reader knows all along—that Ernestine is chaste—Ernestine has made a more important discovery and thereby lost her intellectual innocence. "A happy situation," the narrator tells us in one of her many neat explanatory aphorisms, "is not conducive to reflection." Only when confronted with Henriette's disapproval and forced to make difficult choices does Ernestine understand at last the impossibility of the hopes she unconsciously cherished: "[B]ut how is it, that one experiences such intense anguish in renouncing a hope one did not have?" She must understand too that society is suspicious; that (in Henriette's view, at least) men are vicious; that Clémengis has behaved, if not wickedly, then at least imprudently; and that the physical and emotional ease with which Ernestine related to him and the world is no longer possible. In the shame that replaces her original serenity, she is like Eve after the fall: "[E]xperiencing for the first time at the marquis's arrival an emotion without hint of pleasure, she feared his presence, and felt the desire to hide from him the impulses of her heart." For all her painterly study of Clémengis, she really sees him only after Henriette has enlightened her. "My eyes are open," Ernestine says simply.

Henriette's diatribe about men, delivered in the course of her lengthy conversation with Ernestine, is one of the most stirring formulations in Riccoboni's work: "They claim they were created to guide, sustain, protect a *timid, weak sex*: yet they alone attack it, encourage its timidity, and take advantage of its weakness." Condemnation of the double standard by which men judge themselves and women differently and by which they simultaneously prescribe laws for the "weaker" sex and urge the infringement of those laws is one of Riccoboni's favorite criticisms of contemporary society. Henriette will shortly acknowledge that the constancy of Clémengis makes him virtually unexampled in her experience; he stands with Mylord Rivers, in Riccoboni's last novel, as an exception to the rule. Clémengis nonetheless is insufficiently sensitive to the fragility of a woman's honor, misgauges the tyranny of appearances, and places too much trust in the feckless Mme Duménil; it never enters his head that he could renounce the economic and social advantages for which he has been bred, and at a critical point he allows his sensuality to govern his sensibility. It falls ultimately to Ernestine to deliver lessons in generosity.

Her reward for her exalted disinterestedness is a fairy-tale marriage. But this is virtually the only happy marriage in an otherwise disabused rendering of social and marital arrangements. Skeletal background details about various characters hardly suggest that marriage generally brings satisfaction: the exile of Ernestine's mother was caused by a "worthless husband"; Mme Duménil is an undignified and unhappy companion to her husband; and Clémengis, on the verge of a marriage of convenience with a young woman just emerging from a convent school, deplores the standard arrangement to which he too yields in principle. "[We] shall soon be united," he writes to Ernestine, "without being consulted, with no concern over whether our hearts are disposed to give of themselves." Most telling is the situation of Henriette Duménil: "Lack of wealth, want of beauty, together with a keen wit, made it unlikely she would marry." These aspects of the novel resonate not only with Riccoboni's experience as unwanted daughter of a jealous and tyrannical mother and a bigamous father but also with Riccoboni's own dismal, failed marriage to an irresponsible man.

The triumph of Ernestine's marriage is thus ambiguous and, for some critics, banal. The only character in the text to be designated solely by her first name (because indeed she has no other), Ernestine acquires through marriage a complete and legitimate surname when the marquis refers to her in the closing lines as the future marquise de Clémengis. The erasure of Juliette Catesby's maiden name when she becomes Milady d'Ossery in Riccoboni's third novel, suggesting the eclipse of her subjectivity, has disappointed some feminist critics. But Ernestine's situation is different, since Ernestine can gain security and status only through such acquisition of a name. And since *Ernestine*, unlike *Catesby* and most of Riccoboni's novels, is not told in the heroine's voice, the novel projects all along a mediated form of subjectivity that does not insist on sentiments at the conclusion. *Ernestine* is largely about the difficulty of relations between the sexes, but in its stylized conclusion love wins out over pride, and good sense wins out over rigid social sanctions; a marriage of love prevails over family estates, as it does over concubinage.

The appeal of *The Story of Ernestine* was considerable for generations of readers. Marie Antoinette owned a copy of the original edition (as well as several other works by Riccoboni and even an edition of the complete works). More professional readers noted its classical purity of style and rhythm. The critic Louis de Bachaumont judged it an example of exquisite taste (2: 200; 5 June 1765). The *Correspondance littéraire* saw in it "a most interesting and agreeable little novel," if a bit hurried toward the end. "This woman," the reviewer concluded, "has a good deal of talent. A distinguished tone, an elegant, light, and brisk style will always place her over all the women who have seen fit to get themselves into print of late" (Grimm et al. 435–36; May 1765). The *Bibliothèque universelle des romans*, which published an adaptation of the novel in 1781, called it an example of works that invite rereading not because they are complicated but, rather, because of their exquisite simplicity: "They are the kinds of writings that one devours when they are new and forgets subsequently, because they do not feature strong outlines, and that one enjoys properly only upon rereading" (153). And for the literary historian Jean-François de La Harpe, who wrote at the end of the century, *Ernestine*'s perfection lay in its brevity: "With respect to *Ernestine*, although it is the author's slimmest writing with respect to length, it is her most important for interest and grace. It is a polished piece that alone would suffice a writer. We could call *Ernestine* Madame Riccoboni's jewel" (21).[2]

Ernestine was not only one of Riccoboni's greatest successes (the other being *Lettres de Mylady Juliette Catesby*) but also perhaps her most lasting. Within a year the novel was translated into English, and a dozen years later interest still ran high enough for the Comédie Italienne to attempt an adaptation of it, a comic opera titled *La protégée sans le savoir* (it was performed only once), written by none other than Choderlos de Laclos, author of the great classic *Les liaisons dangereuses*. As discerning an observer as the novelist-educator Félicité de Genlis could declare a half century later that *everyone* had read "the pretty novella called *Ernestine*" (280).

Ernestine's most often cited quality was that elusive one called charm, a trait attributed to the best exemplars of the sentimental vogue. "A charming tale," said the *Gazette littéraire de l'Europe* (March–May 1765: 5). "All the charm that wit and grace can add to tenderness and virtue," said Laclos (758–59).[3] In the mid-nineteenth century the *Revue de Paris* still acknowledged in its subject, although somewhat grudgingly, "a fresh and charmingly simple idea" (Mme M.). And for Julia Kavanagh, author of an 1862 study, the concluding events "only divert us from one of the most charming groups [of characters] Madame Riccoboni ever drew" (17). The charm is neither that of the utterly fanciful (as in a fairy tale) nor that of triumphant jubilation (as in comedy) but that of a slightly moral satisfaction, albeit without illusions, procured by a judicious sort of fictionally immanent justice. Men, it turns out, are not all bad, nor are women always unhappy.

Notes

[1]All quotations from the French are in our translation, unless otherwise indicated—JHS and PS.

[2]The first edition of the *Lycée, ou cours de littérature,* in which La Harpe's critique appears, was in 1798–1804.

[3]In his letter of April 1782 to Riccoboni, Laclos included *Fanni Butlerd* and *Juliette Catesby* in these words of appreciation.

Works Cited

Bachaumont, Louis Petit de, et al. *Mémoires secrets pour servir à l'histoire de la république des lettres en France depuis 1762 jusqu'à nos jours.* 36 vols. London: Adamson, 1777–89.

Bibliothèque universelle des romans. Feb. 1781.

Charrière, Isabelle de. *Letters of Mistress Henley Published by Her Friend.* Trans. Philip Stewart and Jean Vaché. Ed. Joan Hinde Stewart and Philip Stewart. New York: MLA, 1993.

Genlis, Félicité de. *De l'influence des femmes sur la littérature française.* Paris: Maradan, 1811.

Graffigny, Françoise de. *Letters from a Peruvian Woman.* Trans. David Kornacker. Ed. Joan DeJean and Nancy K. Miller. New York: MLA, 1993.

Grimm, Friedrich Melchior, et al. *Correspondance littéraire, philosophique et critique.* Vol. 4. Paris: Longchamps, 1813.

Kavanagh, Julia. *French Women of Letters: Biographical Sketches.* Vol. 2. London: Hurst, 1862.

Kibédi Varga, A. "Le désagrégation de l'idéal classique dans le roman français de la première moitié du dix-huitième siècle." *Studies on Voltaire and the Eighteenth Century.* Vol. 26. Geneva: Institut et Musée Voltaire, 1963. 965–98.

Laclos, Choderlos de. *Œuvres complètes.* Paris: Gallimard, 1979.

La Harpe, Jean-François de. *Cours de littérature.* Vol. 23. Paris: Hiard, 1834.

Mme M. "Mme Riccoboni." *Revue de Paris* 35 (1841): 207.

Nicholls, James C., ed. *Mme Riccoboni's Letters to David Hume, David Garrick, and Sir Robert Liston, 1764–1783. Studies on Voltaire and the Eighteenth Century.* Vol. 149. Oxford: Voltaire Foundation, 1976.

WORKS BY
Marie Riccoboni

Works Published in Her Lifetime

1757   *Lettres de Mistriss Fanni Butlerd*

1758   *Histoire de M. le marquis de Cressy*

1759   *Lettres de Mylady Juliette Catesby à Mylady Henriette Campley, son amie*

1761–64   *Suite de Marianne*

         L'abeille

         L'aveugle

         Lettre de Mme de X... à M. le comte de X...

         Extrait des mémoires du comte de Lipari

         Lettres de la princesse Zelmaïde

1762   *Amélie*

1764   *Histoire de Miss Jenny, écrite et envoyée par elle à Mylady, comtesse de Roscomonde, ambassadrice d'Angleterre à la cour de Dannemark*

1765   *Histoire d'Ernestine*

1767   *Lettres d'Adélaïde de Dammartin, comtesse de Sancerre, à M. le comte de Nancé, son ami*

1768–69   *Nouveau théâtre anglais*

1772   *Lettres d'Elisabeth Sophie de Vallière à Louise Hortense de Canteleu, son amie*

xxiii

1777   *Lettres de Mylord Rivers à Sir Charles Cardigan,*
          entremêlées d'une partie de ses correspondances à
          Londres pendant son séjour en France

1779–80   *Histoire des amours de Gertrude et de Roger*
          Histoire d'Enguerrand, ou rencontre dans la forêt
          des Ardennes
          Histoire d'Aloïse de Livarot
          Histoire de Christine, reine de Suabe

1785   *Lettres de la marquise d'Artigues*

1786   *Histoire de deux jeunes amies*

Modern Editions

Histoire de M. le marquis de Cressy. Ed. Olga Cragg. *Studies on Voltaire and the Eighteenth Century* 266. Oxford: Voltaire Foundation, 1989.

Histoire d'Ernestine. Pref. Colette Piau-Gillot. Paris: Côté-Femmes, 1991.

Histoire du marquis de Cressy. Ed. Alix S. Deguise. Paris: Des Femmes, 1987.

Lettres de Mistriss Fanni Butlerd. Paris: Volland, 1786. Ed. Joan Hinde Stewart. Geneva: Droz, 1979.

Lettres de Mylady Juliette Catesby à Mylady Henriette Campley, son amie. Pref. Sylvain Menant. Paris: Desjonquères, 1983.

Lettres de Mylord Rivers à Sir Charles Cardigan. Ed. Olga Cragg. Geneva: Droz, 1992.

Suite de Marianne. La vie de Marianne. By Marivaux. Ed. Frédéric Deloffre. Paris: Garnier, 1990. 585–627.

SELECTED BIBLIOGRAPHY

André, Arlette. "Le féminisme chez Madame Riccoboni." *Studies on Voltaire and the Eighteenth Century* 193 (1980): 1988–95.

Cazenobe, Colette. "Le féminisme paradoxal de Madame Riccoboni." *Revue d'histoire littéraire de la France* 88 (1988): 23–45.

Cook, Elizabeth Heckendorn. "Going Public: The Letter and the Contract in *Fanni Butlerd.*" *Eighteenth-Century Studies* 24 (1990): 21–45.

Coulet, Henri. "Quelques aspects du roman antirévolutionnaire sous la Révolution." *Revue de l'Université d'Ottawa / University of Ottawa Quarterly* 54.3 (1984): 27–47.

Crosby, Emily. *Une romancière oubliée: Madame Riccoboni.* Paris: Rieder, 1924.

Demay, Andrée. *Marie Jeanne Riccoboni ou de la pensée féministe chez une romancière du XVIIIe siècle.* Paris: La Pensée Universelle, 1977.

Flaux, Mireille. "La fiction selon Mme Riccoboni." *Dix-huitième siècle* 27 (1995): 425–37.

———. *Madame Riccoboni: Une idée du bonheur au féminin au siècle des Lumières.* Lille: U de Lille III, Atelier National de Reproduction des Thèses, 1991.

Hogsett, Alice Charlotte. "Graffigny and Riccoboni on the Language of the Woman Writer." *Eighteenth-Century Women and the Arts.* Ed. Frederick M. Keener and Susan E. Lorsch. New York: Greenwood, 1988. 119–27.

Kavanagh, Julia. *French Women of Letters: Biographical Sketches.* 2 vols. London: Hurst, 1862.

Lanser, Susan. *Fictions of Authority: Women, Writers and Narrative Voice.* Ithaca: Cornell UP, 1992.

Merlant, Joachim. *Le roman personnel de Rousseau à Fromentin.* Paris: Hachette, 1905.

Mooij, Anne Louis Anton. *Caractères principaux et tendances des romans psychologiques chez quelques femmes-auteurs, de Mme Riccoboni à Mme de Souza, 1757–1826.* Groningen: Drukkerij de Waal, 1949.

Nicholls, James C., ed. *Mme Riccoboni's Letters to David Hume, David Garrick, and Sir Robert Liston, 1764–1783.* Studies on Voltaire and the Eighteenth Century 149. Oxford: Voltaire Foundation, 1976.

Piau, Colette. "L'écriture féminine? À propos de Marie Jeanne Riccoboni." *Dix-huitième siècle* 16 (1984): 369–86.

Servien, Michèle. "Madame Riccoboni, vie et œuvre." 2 vols. Diss., U de Paris IV, 1973.

Sol, Antoinette. "Violence and Persecution in the Drawing Room: Subversive Sexual Strategies in Riccoboni's *Miss Juliette Catesby.*" *Public Space of the Domestic Sphere.* Ed. Servanne Woodward. Ontario: Mestengo, 1997. 65–76.

———. "Why Write as a Woman? The Riccoboni-Laclos Correspondence." *Women in French Studies* 3 (1995): 34–44.

Stewart, Joan Hinde. "Aimer à soixante ans: Les lettres de Madame Riccoboni à Sir Robert Liston." *Aimer en France, 1760–1860.* Vol 1. Clermont-Ferrand: Faculté des Lettres et Sciences Humaines de Clermont-Ferrand, 1980. 181–89.

———. *Gynographs: French Novels by Women of the Late Eighteenth Century.* Lincoln: U of Nebraska P, 1993.

———. *The Novels of Madame Riccoboni.* Chapel Hill: North Carolina Studies in the Romance Langs. and Lits., 1976.

Sturzer, Felicia Berger. "Literary Portraits and Cultural Critique in the Novels of Marie Jeanne Riccoboni." *French Studies* 50 (1996): 400–12.

Thomas, Ruth P. "Marie Jeanne Riccoboni." *French Women Writers.* Ed. Eva Martin Sartori and Dorothy Wynne Zimmerman. Westport: Greenwood, 1991. 357–68.

Trousson, Raymond, ed. *Romans de femmes du XVIIIe siècle.* Paris: Laffont, 1996.

Van Dijk, Suzan. *"L'histoire d'Ernestine,* d'après Marie Jeanne Riccoboni et d'après la *Bibliothèque universelle des romans."* *Acts of the Journée Riccoboni, U de Paris–Sorbonne, March 1997.* Forthcoming.

———. "Lire ou broder: Deux occupations féminines dans l'œuvre de Mmes de Graffigny, Riccoboni, et de Charrière." *L'épreuve du lecteur.* Ed. Jan Herman and Paul Pelckmans. Louvain: Peeters, 1995.

———. "Marie-Jeanne Riccoboni en avance sur son époque? Une lecture par l'abbé de La Porte." *Eighteenth-Century Fiction* 8 (1996): 453–64.

Vanpée, Janie. "Dangerous Liaisons 2: The Riccoboni-Laclos Sequel." *Eighteenth-Century Fiction* 9 (1996): 51–70.

Zawisza, Elisabeth. *"Histoire d'Ernestine* de Mme Riccoboni ou l'art de la miniature." *Acts of the Xe Colloque International de la Société d'Analyse de la Topique Romanesque (la SATOR), Johannesburg, September 1996.* Ed. Michèle Weil and Nathalie Ferrand. PU de Montpellier. Forthcoming.

About the Text and Translation

When Denis Humblot, Riccoboni's principal publisher, published *Ernestine* along with short pieces by her in 1765, he included a letter from Riccoboni that said:

> No, assuredly my letters are not finished, they are not even very far along. In vain do you press me; I do not wish to set a time, for fear I will fail to meet it, or feel most uneasy about meeting it: my custom is never to make commitments.
>
> The little story of Ernestine is ready, it is true; I agree to give it to you: my design was to place it elsewhere, but never mind. . . .
>
> With your gentle air and honest disposition, you are tolerably stubborn; since you nag me for this trifle, I do not intend to disappoint you. Print it then, Monsieur Humblot, do as you wish with it: here is the manuscript of Ernestine: I regret it some, since I had not intended it to accompany these sorts of fragments; but nonetheless I leave it to you. I wish you a good day, and good success.
>
> (*Recueil* iv)[1]

To publish this letter was to concede that he was pressing Riccoboni and that she resented the lack of control over completion of her works to her own satisfaction. It appears from this letter that she coughed up *Ernestine* to buy a bit of peace over the next full-length novel Humblot was expecting from her.

The letter apparently spawned several later misunderstandings about the dating of *Ernestine*. The Didot edition of 1814 begins with a "Notice concerning Madame Riccoboni," which seems to place *Ernestine* right after *Catesby*, around 1760:

> *Ernestine* followed *Mylady Catesby*. It is another charming work, the only flaw of which is being too short. La Harpe calls *Ernestine* Madame Riccoboni's jewel; but Madame Riccoboni has many jewels.
>
> Encouraged by the success of these novels, and having furthermore lost the beauties of youth, Madame Riccoboni left the theater in 1761.
>
> (Riccoboni, *Histoire du marquis* xix)

No evidence is adduced for this particular juxtaposition of events. The notice goes on to mention *Amélie* (1762) and the *Lettres de Sancerre* (1767).

A certain Weiss, author of the article on Riccoboni in the Michaud *Biographie universelle*, apparently combines these two sources to situate *Ernestine* between Riccoboni's renunciation of the theater in 1761 and *Amélie*. Weiss makes the following assertion: "Pressed by her editors, she did not get everything she could have out of *Ernestine*'s fine subject. Nevertheless La Harpe considers this little novel as Madame Riccoboni's jewel" (*Biographie* 533). It does not occur to him to specify when the novel might have been published. Doubtless following Weiss, Brissot-Thivars in his own "Notice on Madame Riccoboni" in

1826 assumed that *Histoire d'Ernestine* had in fact preceded *Amélie*:

> In 1762, Madame Riccoboni published *Amélie*; she was, it is said, pressed by publishers; publishers had already harassed her while she was working on the outline of *Ernestine*; it is to their insistence, which hurried the author's work, that its carelessness and the flaws for which critics have reproached these two works are attributed; it is probable that the publishers and the editors had the same objective, which was to take advantage of the public's impatience and curiosity. The speculation paid off; *Amélie* was almost as successful as *Ernestine*.
>
> (Riccoboni, *Œuvres* 1: xviii–xix)

This mistaken dating of *Ernestine* is repeated in the *Nouvelle biographie générale* in 1863 (Morel 154), but in fact no evidence for a date of composition or publication earlier than 1765, or any reason to doubt the sincerity of Riccoboni's published letter to Humblot, has ever been put forward.[2] Nor, in fact, did she in any way justify the interpretation that *Ernestine* was written quickly, much less that her haste accounts for its shortcomings. On the contrary, Riccoboni distinctly states that she refuses to be rushed, but that *Ernestine* is ready. La Harpe himself recognizes it as "a polished piece." Despite so many repetitions of this threadbare story, *Ernestine* was not the victim at all of Humblot's impatience, except in the very limited sense, about which Riccoboni is equally clear, that she had intended to publish it elsewhere. Where, we don't know.

The "fragments" published in 1765 by Humblot were entitled *Recueil de pièces détachées* and included, with *Ernestine*, the *Suite de Marianne, L'abeille, L'aveugle,* and *Lettres de la princesse Zelmaïde.* (Another 1765 edition, brought out in Liège by D. de Boubers, was entitled *Les vrais caractères du sentiment, ou histoire d'Ernestine.*) The same grouping as in the original Humblot edition was used in 1772. *Histoire d'Ernestine* appeared in editions alone or in combination with other works in 1766, 1772, 1814, 1821, 1826, 1828, 1835, 1849 (this edition was reissued in 1863, 1866, 1870), and 1853, and in editions of Riccoboni's collected works in 1773, 1781, 1783, 1786, 1787, 1790, 1792, 1808–09, 1818, and 1826. In 1991 the novel was published by Côté-Femmes (Paris), with a preface by Colette Piau-Gillot.

The present edition is based on the text appearing in volume 5 (pp. 1–86) of the 1786 edition of Riccoboni's complete works (Paris: Volland, 8 vols.), the last to have been corrected by the author. Punctuation has been somewhat modernized, particularly by the addition of quotation marks, the use of which was not current in 1765.

The collection containing *Histoire d'Ernestine* was very soon translated into English,[3] and this same translation may have been used in 1781 when *Ernestine* was combined with stories by other writers in one volume.[4] A further English edition, oddly called *Erestina,* comes, as the title page concedes, "with alterations and additions of the translator," Francis Lathom[5]—a promise the translation fulfills, so it was naturally not very helpful to the present translators.

In our translation, we have applied the general principles used in our earlier edition of Charrière's *Letters of Mistress Henley,* published by the MLA. Accuracy being the principal objective, we have stayed as close as reasonably possible to the vocabulary and sentence structure of the original. The usual problem of handling the opposition between *tu* and *vous* was not at issue here, since the polite Parisians in this novel almost never use the second-person singular. But constructions in *on* and the usual ambiguities of words like *fille* (which can mean "maiden," "girl," "daughter," or "prostitute") still had to be faced with some flexibility and tact. The renderings must be context-specific, and this necessity entails both some risk and the occasional sacrifice of multiple resonance, for semantic echoes are never identical in two languages. Although we have not attempted to imitate eighteenth-century English, we have hoped to respect the period flavor to a certain degree, by eschewing distinctly modern-sounding words and allowing a few mild archaisms.

We wish to thank Mireille Flaux and Michèle Servien for their help; and Alex DeGrand, Larysa Mykyta, Donald S. Petrey, James Rolleston, English Showalter, and Paul Sorum for reading the manuscript and making suggestions. We are especially grateful to Martha Evans and Michael Kandel for their help and encouragement throughout the editing and translating of *Histoire d'Ernestine*.

Notes

[1] "[M]y letters are not finished" refers to *Lettres d'Adélaïde de Dammartin, comtesse de Sancerre*, which was to appear in 1767. When Humblot republished *Ernestine* in 1766, he modified the phrase "I had not intended it to accompany these sorts of fragments" to read: "I had not intended it to stand alone" (Riccoboni, *Histoire d'Ernestine* 4).

[2]Michèle Servien concludes in her painstakingly researched thesis that *Ernestine*, "written during the first trimester of 1765, corresponded to Madame Riccoboni's preoccupations of that time" (141).

[3]*The Continuation of the Life of Marianne, to Which Is Added the History of Ernestine, with Letters and Other Miscellaneous Pieces*. London: Becket and DeHondt, 1766.

[4]*Select Novels Containing The Blind Boy* [by James Kinney], Indian Letters, The Distressed Orphan; or, Adventures of Ernestine. London: Lane, 1781.

[5]The book, undated (1803?), was published in Norwich by J. Payne, Longman, and Rees.

Works Cited

Biographie universelle ancienne et moderne. Vol. 37. Paris: Michaud, 1824.

Morel, Jean. "Riccoboni." *Nouvelle biographie générale*. Vol. 42. Paris: Didot, 1863. 153–55.

Riccoboni, Marie. *Histoire d'Ernestine*. Paris: Humblot, 1766.

———. *Histoire du marquis de Cressy suivie d'Ernestine*. Paris: Didot, 1814.

———. *Œuvres*. 8 vols. Paris: Brissot-Thivars, 1826.

———. *Recueil de pièces détachées*. Paris: Humblot, 1765.

Servien, Michèle. "Madame Riccoboni, vie et œuvre." Vol. 1. Diss. U of Paris IV, 1973.

MARIE RICCOBONI

The Story of Ernestine

A foreigner, young and attractive but poor and un-known, who had been in Paris only three months, occupied two ground-floor rooms in the Faubourg Saint-Antoine[1]; she lived off what she could make embroidering. As she was returning one evening after selling some of her work, she was taken ill at the entrance to her house. Efforts to aid and revive her were vain; she expired without coming to her senses, or giving any sign of consciousness.

The women living nearby, frightened by this terrible mischance, filled her sorry abode with cries and exclamations; they called to each other, repeating back and forth, "Christine, alas! poor Christine!"

A lady[2] whose garden was bordered by the wall of the house from which this commotion arose, drawn by the desire to be of use to those who were lamenting so loudly,

---

[1]*Faubourg* means "suburb." The Faubourg Saint-Antoine lay to the east of Paris, just beyond the Bastille, and was a heavily populated workers' neighborhood known particularly for the furniture and dec-orating trades.

[2]*Une bourgeoise*: not a working woman but a member of the profes-sional or merchant class.

went over in person to learn the cause of their clamor, and was informed of it. As she was listening, her eyes fixed upon a little girl of about three or four; this innocent creature was weeping beside the deceased, calling to her, pulling at her dress, and crying: "Mother, wake up! Mother, won't you wake up?"

The heart of the compassionate neighbor was moved by this spectacle. She came forward, took the child in her arms, caressed her, and dried her tears. The child's beauty redoubled her sympathy. She sent for an officer of the law and provided money to have the stranger buried. After fulfilling all the formalities required for her plan to take care of the young orphan, she took her by the hand and led her to her home.

The name of the woman whose good heart manifested itself in this act of humanity was Madame Dufresnoi. The widow of a modest merchant, she had just come to an agreement with her husband's family, contenting herself with an annuity of three thousand livres,[3] and abandoning rather considerable claims against the inheritance of his children by a first marriage. This generous action procured her the satisfaction of seeing suitably established

---

[3]*Livre* is often translated as "pounds," but we retain the French word (used also in English at the time) because the French livre was worth far less than the pound sterling. Three thousand livres represents a rather minimal standard of living, above poverty but devoid of luxuries, including servants.

the daughters of an honest man whose memory she cherished.[4]

The little foreign girl's name was Ernestine. She was German, and appeared not to be of common birth. She could speak French only with difficulty. After much questioning, it was understood from what she said that a worthless husband had forced the unfortunate Christine to leave her home and her fatherland, and nothing more was ever learned of her.

Ernestine mourned her mother, asking often for her in the first few days after her death. Then she forgot her, grew, developed, became beautiful: her svelte, lithe stature, dark eyes full of fire, lovely ash-blond hair, white, straight teeth, a sweet and gentle smile, grace, an unspoiled mind, made her at twelve a charming girl. She received a simple education, learned to cherish virtue, to regard honor as the supreme law; but as she lived a very secluded life, her mind could not extend itself; she acquired no familiarity with society, and long remained in that tranquil and dangerous ignorance of vices that, keeping fear and sad distrust far from our mind, disposes us to judge others by ourselves, and causes us to regard all humans as creatures disposed to cherish us and be helpful to us.

---

[4]That is, the family disposed of a large enough sum to provide the daughters with a dowry.

Madame Dufresnoi, tenderly attached to this young person, sadly envisaged the situation in which she might one day find herself: what would Ernestine do were her friend's death to leave her without assistance? Though unable to secure her future, she wished at least to give her a skill that could provide for her life's needs and even a little luxury. She chose miniature painting,[5] and brought in a painter to teach her drawing. Ernestine, attentive, intelligent, and docile, applied herself, manifested considerable gifts, cultivated them, advanced, and was showing promise of becoming proficient, when Madame Dufresnoi, taken with a malignant fever, was suddenly at death's door; she died the fifth day after falling ill.

Henriette Duménil, sister of the painter who was giving instruction to Ernestine, was friendly with Madame Dufresnoi; they lived near each other and visited together fairly frequently. Henriette was about thirty years of age; having been raised by one of her relatives, a woman of wealth who was well known in society, she combined a most amiable natural disposition with the affability acquired by the habit of mixing with a refined circle. Lack of wealth, want of beauty, together with a keen wit, made it unlikely she would marry. The goodness of her character,

---

[5]The art of painting in very small dimensions, such as medallion portraits or scenes on small boxes. Such portraits could be kept in lockets or otherwise serve as love tokens.

the honesty of her morals, and her known probity attached sincere and faithful friends to her.

Henriette stayed with Madame Dufresnoi throughout her illness, and when the time had come, she wrested the disconsolate Ernestine from her bedside, took her to her relative's house, and shut herself up with her in her apartment. She allowed her tears to flow, shed some of her own, and granted her the kindness a grieving heart needs: the freedom to lament, to grieve, which insensitive or clumsy consolers think they are supposed to restrain, contain, even take from us! Such zeal is akin to harshness: serene reasoning, empty words, cold reflections wound a soul overwhelmed by the weight of its anguish. Now why, for what reason try to persuade an unfortunate that the dart piercing her flesh should leave scarcely a trace of its passage?

Henriette, named executrix in Madame Dufresnoi's will, faithfully discharged that duty: the furniture and effects were sold for Ernestine's benefit, and the sum of eight thousand livres that they brought in was invested in her name. A decent and suitable refuge had to be found for her; Henriette could not keep her. Monsieur Duménil, attached to his pupil, persuaded his wife to take her in. This worthy man contented himself with a very modest payment, promising to cultivate her gifts and enable her to support herself through her talent. Ernestine gratefully accepted his offers, and two months after the death of her benefactress, Henriette saw her to her brother's house.

Ernestine's anguish was deeper than would have been expected from someone of her age: she mourned Madame Dufresnoi, mourned her bitterly, yet did not imagine all the consequences of what, in her, she had lost. The cause of her tears was the regret of being forever separated from a kind, good, and attentive woman, from a tender, indulgent companion. Madame Duménil's character was not the sort to compensate her for her first friend: insouciant, whimsical, even foolish, she laughed at everything, took interest in nothing, confused sadness with ill humor, and considered anyone who was sorrowful as merely tedious.

This woman, age twenty-six, had a decided taste for dissipation and amusement; most constrained in her spending, she could neither afford the pleasures she craved, nor resign herself to doing without them. She sought the means of satisfying her desires despite her meager fortune, and became the complaisant friend of several women of less than the most scrupulous conduct.[6] Monsieur Duménil, good, simple, absorbed by his art, while taking care of his delicate lungs and his frail and frequently languishing health, let his wife live as she saw fit. An elderly and reasonable housekeeper looked after

---

[6]In other words, she assisted them in their amorous adventures.

the household, and kept good watch on her master. Madame Duménil went to the theater, dined out, came home late, slept through part of the day; and as her husband made no objection, nothing obliged her to rein herself in. Monsieur Duménil's pupil, immersed in her study, saw her scarcely twice a month, and when they spoke, it was politely, but with mutual indifference.

Ernestine spent three years with her master, during which time the peaceful uniformity of her life was untroubled. When she had reached the degree of perfection to which Monsieur Duménil could guide her, she was able, thanks to her inborn taste, far to surpass his lessons; he noted this with pleasure. As he was often ill, unable to work himself, he took it upon himself to publicize his pupil's talents: he prevailed on several of his friends to let her do their portraits, and these first efforts began to create a reputation for her.

One day as she was alone in Monsieur Duménil's studio, putting the finishing touches on a miniature he was supposed to have ready soon, she heard the door open, turned about, and saw a man whose distinguished attire and demeanor could attract attention. As a consequence of Ernestine's application to her work, she was merely struck to perceive him as the original of the portrait on which she was working. She greeted him without a word; a simple nod, a gesture of the hand invited him to be seated; he silently complied. Ernestine fixed her eyes on him, then lowered them to the miniature, and for a good while her eyes alternately surveyed the amiable gentleman and his image.

This coincidence occasioned as much pleasure as surprise in the marquis de Clémengis. He had come to urge Monsieur Duménil to give him the portrait, which a lady impatiently awaited. He had expected to find the painter in the studio where he usually worked; to find a charming girl in his place, busy observing his features, so perfectly absorbed in studying his image that she seemed to enjoy looking at it: this was a sort of adventure, simple but agreeable, which amused him, intrigued him, and made a very keen impression on him.

While Ernestine continued to compare the original with the copy, the marquis admired the grace that marked her whole person. Impatient to hear her speak, he hoped her education and wit would correspond to such a predisposing face. He was on the point of addressing her, when Monsieur Duménil entered, and apologized at length for his inability to deliver the portrait. The marquis, already less in a hurry to give it away, interrupted the painter, and wishing to obtain once more the satisfaction of seeing Ernestine's eyes fix on his, he feigned displeasure with it, found shortcomings of resemblance, of design, of coloration; and since his faultfinding was random, Monsieur Duménil's young pupil could not help but laugh at his observations.

The marquis entreated her to examine closely whether he was in error. She consented. He placed himself before her, and after giving the matter her entire attention, Ernestine judged the copy perfect. Monsieur de Clémengis insisted; she did not yield. The sound of her voice, the aptness of her expressions, a touch of petulance provoked by the marquis's false remarks, utterly enchanted him. He requested a copy of his portrait, and insisted it be entirely by Ernestine's hand. The painter so promised. Monsieur de Clémengis, finally out of pretexts for prolonging the pleasure of remaining with Ernestine, regretfully left the studio, and Monsieur Duménil, seeing him to his carriage, satisfied his curiosity by acquainting him with his pupil's story.

The man whom chance had just set before Ernestine's eyes possessed not only a thousand exterior attractions but also a rare, perhaps singular, character. Monsieur de Clémengis, a descendant of an ancient and distinguished family, was not born to wealth: his expectations of fortune hinged upon the revision of a lawsuit that had been pursued for nearly a century by his forebears. His good luck had placed in the ministry one of his close relatives. Since this powerful man was fond of him, the marquis enjoyed all the advantages attached to favor; but he did not abuse it. More sensitive than vain, more generous than ostentatious, his noble and delicate soul prized grandeur and wealth for the power they possessed to make people happy. A gentle and tender disposition led him to desire friends: he found flatterers, rendered them services, but disdained them; he discovered selfish motivation in all the people blandishing him. Love itself gave him no unalloyed pleasures: if for a moment he tasted the satisfaction of believing he was chosen and preferred, unwanted requests, pressing and reiterated solicitations soon let him perceive that his influence was more attractive than his person. He had long been seeking a heart that could love him for himself, and was distressed to find none.

During the time Ernestine was at work on the copy of the marquis's portrait, she allowed him to visit every morning, attributing his assiduity solely to the motive that served as his pretext. Nothing had disposed her mind to be on guard; she was unaware of the danger to which the sight of an amiable man could expose her, and the simplicity of her thoughts left her in complete security. A person who has never felt the desire to please can please for a long while without being aware of it, and love that is concealed so resembles friendship that it is easy to mistake one for the other.

Monsieur de Clémengis, each day more under Ernestine's charm, was dismayed to observe that the work was advancing; in order to preserve the pleasure of calling often at the painter's, he resolved he would learn an art he was beginning to like. Monsieur Duménil, already infirm, and destined to die soon of an incurable disease, was rarely in good enough health to direct the marquis's efforts; his charming pupil was entrusted with this charge. She showed this docile schoolboy how to hold and guide his crayons, teaching him to imitate the lines she herself drew; she often laughed at his clumsiness, sometimes she scolded him, accused him of lacking understanding, complained of his absentmindedness and, pointing to two young girls who were drawing in the same room, she chided him for profiting less from her lessons than those children did.

Never had the marquis spent more agreeable moments; the joy of familiar conversation with a girl of sixteen, unaware of her own beauty, modest without affectation, amusing, lively, playful, on whom his rank, his fortune, or his influence imposed no deference; who allowed herself to express natural joy when he appeared; whose innocence and naïveté made all her sentiments free and true; to be seated close to her, to call her his mistress,[7] to see her assert a kind of authority over him; to endeavor to satisfy her, to please her while admitting to no such intent, to flatter himself that he succeeded in doing so: this was such

_____

[7]Feminine of "master," which is what a tutor is called.

an interesting occupation for the marquis de Clémengis that he gradually lost his ability to enjoy all the vain amusements of which idleness attempts to make pleasures.

Madame Duménil, obliged by her husband's unfortunate condition to remain at home, perceived the marquis's love; she showed him an indulgent humor, had long conversations with him, gained his confidence, espoused his point of view, and, pleased by his generosity, she began to treat Ernestine as a person whose company she was sorry to have long neglected. She paid her tender compliments, tried to understand her needs, her desires; endeavored to satisfy them. With each day Ernestine's situation grew more congenial and agreeable; her gratitude made her forget this woman's long coldness; she was touched by her kindnesses and forgave her a flightiness of mind from which, after all, she had never suffered. When others' flaws do us no harm, it is rare that we find them very shocking. As Madame Duménil was cheerful and indulgent, and as a secret self-interest committed her to making Ernestine love her, she easily inspired friendship in an affectionate girl who thought it was to her she owed the luxuries she was beginning to enjoy.

Monsieur Duménil was approaching his last hours; the inevitability of his death caused his tender pupil to weep, and the marquis frequently found her all in tears. Mixed with her sorrow was an intense anxiety: Henriette, who had left two months earlier for Brittany,[8] suddenly ceased giving news of herself; Ernestine missed her at a time when her counsel was becoming needful. Ernestine wrote to her several times and received no reply. This silence distressed her: was her friend ill? Was she neglecting to inform her what she should do following her master's death? She brought this up with Madame Duménil, who reassured her about Henriette's health, and scolded her gently for seeking from Henriette advice of which she had no need. "Do you think me capable of deserting you?" she said to her in an affectionate tone of voice. "Do you intend to leave me? No, my dear Ernestine, we shall never part; you shall share my fortune, it is perhaps considerable enough to make you happy: I have resources unknown to you. Say nothing of this secret; cease troubling yourself, and have no more regret for Henriette's advice; it could only disrupt the plan that is in place for your happiness."

Such words, oft repeated, dispelled Ernestine's anxiety, but her heart was wounded by Henriette's forgetfulness. Henriette had promised when she left ever to take an interest in her welfare, and to find a refuge for her should Henriette's brother die. Ernestine was unable to reconcile

---

[8] We are to understand that the "rich relative," later referred to as a cousin and, by Madame Duménil, as a "distant relative," owns an estate in Brittany, where she and Henriette occasionally go for an extended stay.

such cold behavior with Henriette's character; but her growing attachment to Madame Duménil slowly attenuated this sorrow and, though unintentionally, the marquis himself helped her to think of other things.

It would soon be time for Monsieur de Clémengis to depart: the regiment he commanded had just gone over into Italy, and he must soon leave to join it. Ernestine noticed his sadness, despite his efforts to conceal it. Wistful and anxious, he maintained a mournful silence; his change of mood surprised her, and his absentmindedness irritated her. His lesson time was spent in sighing, in complaining of an inner anguish, a hidden and violent sorrow. Ernestine felt moved by the condition she saw him in; she inquired sympathetically into its cause, and urged him to confide in her: but seeing that her queries made him sadder still, she ceased questioning him, though she did not cease worrying about his sorrow. She thought about it all the time, impatiently awaiting the hour when the marquis would come; she fixed on him curious and inquisitive eyes, and always finding him somber, she lowered them, fearful of encountering his gaze, dared not say a word, and asked herself: "What is the matter? I believed he was so happy; is he no longer?"

While she was sharing the marquis's anguish, unaware of its origin, he was attending to the generous purpose of establishing her future, of making it happy and independendent. Madame Duménil, who had been promised a considerable reward to pretend it was she who showered on her friend the things she would enjoy thanks to Monsieur de Clémengis, was unable to understand the strange conduct of so generous and so discreet an admirer.

"How can you hope to touch Ernestine's heart," she would say to him, "if you conceal the passion she inspires in you? You give her riches, and wish her to be unaware of your love and favors?" "Oh, may she forever remain unaware of these favors," he replied. "My intention is to please her, and not to seduce her; to make her free, and never to constrain or enslave her; I like to see her showing me innocent affection, attaching herself to me without design, without intention, without fear, without expectation. Her eyes have expressed sympathy since she perceived my sadness: perhaps she loves me! Should I dictate to this charming girl? If I made her feel grateful, I should interfere with her inclination, I should lose the delight of believing I possess a heart that cherishes me for myself alone."

Monsieur de Clémengis then repeated to Madame Duménil all the instructions he had already given her concerning the conduct she was to adopt after her husband's death. She promised to conform to his wishes, to keep his secret faithfully, and to inform him in her letters of Ernestine's thoughts on the change in her situation. A few days after their conversation, Monsieur de Clémengis was obliged to depart. The following day, at the hour when he ordinarily came to Ernestine's, she received from him a very ornate case, containing the portrait Monsieur Duménil had made of the marquis, and this note:

The Marquis de Clémengis to Ernestine

I leave you, my charming mistress; an unavoidable duty forces me to forgo the delight of seeing you, of profiting from your attention and your kind-nesses. But I shall not forget your lessons: recalling them will be my only consolation during a long and sad absence. In your leisure moments, do me the favor of looking at this portrait, and copying it; multiply the image of a friend whose heart is ten-derly attached to you; preserve his memory, and hope sometimes to see him again.

Ernestine felt shocked and saddened as she read this note. Why was Monsieur de Clémengis going away with-out taking leave of her, without telling her he was going? She read his letter several times, still appalled by his un-explained conduct; little by little she mellowed, her anger giving way to her sense of loss. Seeing the marquis, talk-ing with him, spending long hours with him had become a pleasant habit for her. What a deprivation! She was los-ing even the pleasure of expecting him.

Her tearful eyes fixed upon the portrait; she studied it a long while; but as she was no longer examining it as an artist, she found that Monsieur de Clémengis had been right to object to this piece of work. "Those are his features," she said to herself, "his physiognomy; but where is his soul, where the vivacity of that countenance? Where are the gentle eyes that express such friendship? How many handsome traits are overlooked! Is this his delicate, tender smile, his kind, grand demeanor? Where are all the graces of which I perceive scarcely a faint suggestion?" As she spoke, Ernestine pushed away all the drawings on her table, looked for her crayons; and filled with the thought of the marquis, was persuaded she could trace a more exact image of him from memory.

This absorbing labor was interrupted some days later by the death of poor Duménil. Ernestine, tenderly attached to this man, sincerely mourned him. His widow, impatient to get away from a place apt to inspire sadness, a sentiment she feared, hastened to put one of her relatives in charge of her affairs, and as soon as decency allowed she betook herself with Ernestine to a charming house three leagues from Paris.[9] Several menservants, anticipating their arrival, came to greet them and looked to their every need.

Ernestine still wept; she constantly remembered the kindness and friendship her master had always shown her. Nevertheless, the cheerful and magnificent sight of this beautiful spot suspended her sorrow; the apartments, the

---

[9]A league is about five kilometers.

gardens, the smell and brilliant colors of the flowers, all overwhelmed her senses, delighted her eyes. "Whoever could have lent you this agreeable lodging?" she said to her friend. "The people who live here must be very happy!"

"If being free to live here seems like happiness to you," replied Madame Duménil, "enjoy it, my dear friend, and fear not to lose it: I am now in possession of a rather considerable fortune, of which this lovely property is a part, and you are mistress of it." Then she recounted a little story, cleverly contrived to make it appear that her marriage, contracted against her family's wishes, had deprived her of her property as long as her husband was alive.

Nothing disposed Ernestine to doubt this woman's sincerity; unfamiliar with both the law and the customs, she believed her unhesitatingly, congratulated her on the happy change in her situation, and felt deeply moved by Madame Duménil's repeated promises to share with her all the pleasures of her new status.

To please her friend, Ernestine was obliged to occupy the handsomest apartment, accept rich presents, accept the attentions of a chambermaid who was there to serve her alone; she had to allow herself to be dressed in style. Madame Duménil was in charge of her daily schedule, and absolutely insisted that a part of her time be reserved for her toilet. Ernestine learned how to enhance her charms by every means that could lend them brilliance.

Little by little this art became easy and agreeable; she liked, even loved, the way she looked, but it was with a moderation that for her was like a natural gift. A dancing master came to show her how to develop the graces of her person; she was given music lessons, and her lithe hands soon got used to running over the keys of a harpsichord; a perfect ear led her in little time to complement their harmony with the sounds of her agile voice. The desire to please Madame Duménil contributed greatly to these advances; often she was also inspired by the pleasure of thinking that the marquis de Clémengis, when he returned, would find her more refined, more amiable, more worthy of his friendship.

When he left Ernestine, this tactful admirer had intended to write to her often; but as he experienced extreme difficulty in doing so without pouring out all his heart's affection, he contented himself with receiving letters from Madame Duménil: they informed him each week of Ernestine's health and occupations; he was ecstatic to learn that she used her every free moment to begin copies of his portrait, or to retouch the one she was insisting on painting without a model.

Two people who think differently do not while enjoying the same advantages find themselves equally happy. Madame Duménil, constrained by her promises, often missed her former friends and the bustling life of the city;

her only amusements were long rides: a fine coach and most handsome team allowed her to wander through the surrounding countryside. Sometimes she regretted having committed herself to a conduct so ill suited to her taste; but the advantages her compliance gained her, and the hope of returning to Paris at the onset of winter, helped her bear the boredom of her isolation.

Ernestine, accustomed to seclusion, lived perfectly content; everything in nature seemed to present an agreeable and interesting spectacle: the first rays of sunrise, the evening of a fine day, the woods, the meadows, the songs of the birds, the varied fruits of the land, offered her untroubled mind either objects of pleasure, or the subject of a tender reverie. Her inclination for Monsieur de Clémengis quickened her heart without troubling it, and caused her to enjoy some of the sweetness sentiment gives, without mixing with it the violent agitation that arises from passions. She hoped to see the marquis again, but an impatient ardor did not turn this desire into painful longing. In this tranquil position, what could engage Ernestine to lift her sights beyond appearances? A happy situation is not conducive to reflection; why seek to understand the cause of the happiness one enjoys? Well-being seems a natural state; its interruption troubles us, stirs us up; misfortune instructs us, extends our thoughts, makes our soul restless and our mind active, because suffering makes us seek within ourselves the strength to bear it, or resources to be free from it.

From the moment the campaign opened, peace talks were well along, and the armies' orders were only to keep watch on each other; toward the middle of the summer they received the order to separate, and our troops crossed back over the mountains. The marquis de Clémengis, kept in Turin by illness, did not reach Paris until early in the fall. Once he had discharged himself of his most pressing duties, he yielded to the desire to see the object of his affection again, and set out for the cheerful abode that his generosity had turned into Ernestine's estate.

She was alone when the marquis was announced; at his name, she uttered a cry of joy, rose, ran to greet him, asked him a thousand questions, and ingenuously betrayed all the pleasure she felt in seeing him again.

Moved, overwhelmed by this greeting, Monsieur de Clémengis said nothing for a moment; he studied Ernestine with as much astonishment as satisfaction. In his presence she had always appeared in proper but simple attire, owing her radiance to her youth, to her regular features, to her natural attractiveness; her charms now heightened by a thousand new graces, her easy carriage, her noble face, that imposing dignity the beauty of which is highlighted by innocence, inspired in Monsieur de Clémengis as much respect as surprise. It was as if he were seeing this charming girl for the first time; she seemed to him born to the station in which his generosity had placed her. Adorned with his gifts and surrounded with his favors, she owed him no gratitude, was unaware of her obligations; there was nothing to subjugate or humiliate her in the eyes of a man who, far from daring to boast of his attentions, was unwilling for them to be apparent, and often questioned himself to be sure he had not himself mistaken the motive that disposed him to such acts.

For several days, the marquis maintained a timid and embarrassed demeanor in Ernestine's presence; he hesitated when he called her his mistress, he had difficulty resuming with her the familiar, gay tone of their early conversations. Little by little his position became uncomfortable. Prior to his departure, when he had been solely occupied with the desire to please, his doubt with respect to the sentiments he inspired had left him enough strength to conceal his own; but to perceive Ernestine's affection, and not dare to appear to share it, to read in her tender eyes the sweetest expressions of love, and hold his tongue! What constraint, what torture for a passionate lover,[10] who was finally enjoying something so long wished for: to be loved, really loved!

---

[10]This word (*amant*) in classical French means only "a man enamored" or "suitor."

His fortune, still hinging on a dispute that was difficult to conclude;[11] the necessity of currying the favor of a relative whose support deserved his gratitude;[12] society, its preconceived notions[13]—everything created an insurmountable barrier between Ernestine and him. He did not dream of breaching it, nor did the honesty of his heart, the nobility of his principles, allow him to defile a girl worthy of esteem, and impose a shameful price on gifts to which she had not laid claim. To deprive himself of the pleasure of seeing her was a means of recovering his tranquillity, but the harshness of this means was repugnant to him. If at times he was prepared to make himself grieve, the certainty of being loved restrained him: how could he bring himself to inflict sorrow on the amiable, affectionate Ernestine! To avoid her, flee her, she who in the simplicity of her heart became daily more attached to him! What would she think of such a bizarre and cruel friend? What impression would that give her?

---

[11]Because marriage contracts often contained complex provisions regarding the husband's and wife's (and eventually the children's) respective portions of the family capital, suits involving contested wills were common and could drag on for years (in this case, the suit has dragged on for decades). Thus Clémengis's family has not yet recovered its full inheritance, and will not unless and until the inheritance is released by a court.

[12]Clémengis has no living parents, but, as we shall see later, his uncle, whose heir he will be, serves as head of the family.

[13]The aristocracy, which considered marriage an alliance between families, did not countenance mésalliance, or marrying below one's rank, and even less marrying someone who had no family.

Would she scorn him for his inconstancy; would she be affected by it? Yes, without a doubt: he could not fail to recognize that his presence inspired joy in Ernestine; oh! how could he take that from her, when it had perhaps become necessary to her very happiness?

This last consideration exerted such power over the mind of Monsieur de Clémengis that it fixed his resolutions. His conduct with Ernestine in no way changed; she perceived in him nothing but a sincere, devoted, indulgent friend, eager to arrange entertainment for her, and content to be allowed to share in it.

The moments they spent together, as avowed friends but secretly in love, flew by quickly: the desire to please each other, tender services, delicate attentions, sustained the inexpressible charm of this intimate and delightful relationship. Ernestine savored its sweetness without fear or worry; but so great a happiness was to be cruelly disrupted, and the time was coming when it would be destroyed by the loss of the happy ignorance that was making it possible.

Madame Duménil, no judge of character, had no knowledge of either the sentiments or the true intentions of Monsieur de Clémengis. By agreeing to assist his designs, she hoped to share in the pleasures with which a prodigal lover would surround his mistress; an open house, abundant company, entertaining suppers, and continual festivities filled her mind with the most cheerful prospects. Disappointed in this expectation, she took it badly: she complained to the marquis of the tedious isolation in which she was living, warned him that she could no longer bear it, and threatened to leave Ernestine if she stayed in the country over the winter.

It was not the design of Monsieur de Clémengis to leave Ernestine there. He had had a house furnished for her in Paris; but since he did not intend to introduce his friend to society, he regretted placing her in the hands of a woman so unreasonable: he must either satisfy Madame Duménil or separate her from Ernestine. Renewed largesse and many blandishments appeased Madame Duménil; she returned to Paris, and escorted Ernestine to the Faubourg Saint-Germain, to a house that was not roomy, but very ornate.[14] Two days after their arrival, she brought to Ernestine's dressing table several jewels intended for her and a casket filled with precious stones.

Ernestine was touched by this present, which she took for another sign of Madame Duménil's solicitous friendship, but she was not dazzled by its magnificence. She was becoming accustomed to wealth, to ostentation; and as she did not wish to provoke envy, she was in no way

---

[14]The Faubourg Saint-Germain was a newly developed section to the west of the Church of Saint-Germain-des-Prés. In stark contrast to the Faubourg Saint-Antoine, where the story begins, it was known for the sumptuous homes of foreigners and upper nobility.

inclined to attach to the possession of these brilliant baubles the value that ordinary women do.

Madame Duménil urged her to put them on; and remembering that the marquis was in Versailles, she lost no time taking advantage of his absence to take Ernestine to the Opera.[15] Her purpose was to inspire in her a taste for the pleasures she herself preferred, and force Monsieur de Clémengis to allow her the liberty to enjoy them.

The newness of this scene completely absorbed Ernestine's attention; she failed to notice that the gaze of a crowd of spectators was drawn toward her, enchanted at her sight and surprised not to know her.[16] Elegant attire, hardly any rouge, great modesty, Madame Duménil's decent figure and her young companion's noble air made them pass for women freshly arrived from the provinces: all eyes fixed on Ernestine. When she left her loge, she was quickly surrounded and almost crushed by the indiscreet curiosity of a swarm of those importunate boys who, released too early to their own supervision,[17] are of-

---

[15]Officially called the Académie Royale de Musique, the Opera was one of three official theaters, the other two being the Comédie Française and the Théâtre Italien. It performed at the Palais Royal, although a fire there in 1763 forced it to relocate to the Tuileries until 1770.

[16]This passage is reminiscent of the surprise of the Prince de Clèves when he first sees a young beauty whom he does not know—and whom he will soon marry (Marie Madeleine de La Fayette, La princesse de Clèves, 1678).

[17]Young men who should still be under a tutor's supervision.

ten hard-pressed to know what to do, and are always a bother to others.

When she reached the foot of the stairway, where several ladies were awaiting their carriages, Ernestine recognized among them Mademoiselle Duménil, who she thought was still in Brittany. Upon seeing her she cried out, cut through the crowd, ran up to her, and embraced her, repeating, "Henriette, my dear Henriette!"—this was the effect of an impulse so prompt that her companion could neither prevent nor arrest it.

Henriette, embarrassed, far from responding to Ernestine's caresses, seemed to be trying to evade them, and pushed her gently away. "Whatever can this mean, Mademoiselle? This is hardly the time or place," she said to her. "Why now this feigned urgency after forgetting for so long? Let me be, I beg you: everything separates us now, and you surely do not regret the loss of a useless friend."

"The loss of a friend!" repeated Ernestine. "And why is that? How have I lost her? How is this, my dear Henriette, do you no longer love me? You admit that you no longer love me!" "I pity you, Mademoiselle," said Henriette; "that is still a way of loving you, of loving you as much as the present difference in our sentiments can allow." And looking at her sorrowfully: "Poor, amiable child," she added softly, "is this really you? How dazzling! But what a poor substitute for the sparkle that shone in my brother's innocent pupil." Then, as one of her companions was calling her to leave, she followed her, leaving Ernestine stunned, perplexed and nearly unable to move.

Madame Duménil had not dared to come near her sister-in-law. On the way back, some anxiety caused her to maintain silence; she waited for Ernestine to speak, intending to gauge from that what Henriette had said. It seemed to her impossible that such a short exchange could have led to great enlightenment. But her friend merely sighed and held her peace; and the consternation she observed in Ernestine made her position most awkward.

As she repeated Henriette's phrases to herself, attempting to grasp their meaning, Ernestine was engulfed in the kind of painful reverie where the flurry of thoughts prevents perceiving and dwelling upon any single one. "Henriette pities me," she said finally; *"everything separates us! The favors you have showered upon me offended her eyes; their sparkle does not befit her brother's pupil! Poor girl!*[18] she cried out. Well, why this compassion, so different from the compassion I used to make her feel? Alas, I have always inspired pity; why does this sentiment now humiliate me? Cast at a tender age into the arms of Providence, taken in by beneficent hands, I owed my subsistence and

---

[18]Italics, here and subsequently, are a typographical convention indicating the reprise of words previously heard or read—although, as in this case, the quotation sometimes is only approximate.

my education to Madame Dufresnoi's generous friendship; Henriette, the trustee of her last kindnesses, did not cease to think well of me when she secured them for me: why do your gifts diminish me in her eyes? Have I been wrong to accept them? Doubtless so: luxury and wealth do not befit me; this borrowed splendor can attract attention to me, remind people of my original situation, dispose envy to turn it into a reproach; for all I know, the poor have no right to raise themselves up; the obscurity of a simple, active life is perhaps their only lot: when one subsists on a friend's favors, everything accepted in excess of one's needs can be ridiculous and despicable."

"Oh, what do you care about Henriette's thoughts?" replied Madame Duménil. "Are you beholden to her? Does that haughty, scornful woman hold rights to you? How would she dare find fault with you for accepting my gifts, when she herself owes everything to the affection of a distant relative? You have much offended me by rushing to greet her; she has always hated me. But since her brother's death, I have had the pleasure of vexing her: she meant to interfere with my conduct and dictate yours, but by closing my door to her,[19] I was able to free myself from her tyranny. She is annoyed with me, I know that: how

---

[19]She refers to a conventional means of refusing to see someone: the person being called on has the servants tell the caller that he or she is not at home.

31

could she forgive me for having made you happy without consulting her about the means of securing your future, without entrusting to her arrangements that the austerity of her principles would have led her to reject?"

"You closed your door to Henriette!" cried Ernestine in surprise. "Dear Lord, what are you telling me?" "Why should you be angry?" replied Madame Duménil. "What is there for you to regret? If I deprive you of a friend, will you not recover one in me? After what I have done for you, I am astonished to find you so attached to another. Enjoy without worry this luxury *that offends the eyes* of Mademoiselle Duménil; and if chance again places before your own eyes a person so disagreeable to mine, avoid speaking to her: you owe me this much deference, and I require it of your friendship."

Ernestine dared not press for the explanations she desired; she was sad and upset all evening long. Nighttime increased her anxiety; a thousand reflections arose in her mind. Why had Madame Duménil always assured her that her sister-in-law was away? What had given rise to such willful, powerful hatred? During Monsieur Duménil's life, the two women did not seek each other's company, but they were together rather often. How could Henriette have objected to arrangements advantageous to her friend, she who so many times had wished she were rich and could share her fortune with her dear ward! She was being called stern and haughty: did these epithets fit Mademoiselle Duménil's indulgent inclination and gentle humor? Ernestine sensed some mystery in her companion's conduct; a vague suspicion aroused her mistrust and inspired in her a sort of fear; still she attempted to calm herself, to shake off the memory of this encounter, to give Madame Duménil a token of her attachment and gratitude by conforming to her will. But how could she bear the doubt in which this would leave her? She thought she had detected scorn and indignation in Mademoiselle Duménil's eyes; misled by a false report, her friend perhaps believed her guilty of fostering the discord between her sister[20] and herself. This last thought rekindled the desire to hear Henriette's side of things; and as Ernestine was not at all in the habit of resisting her soul's impulses, she gave in to them, awaited daylight impatiently, arose as soon as it appeared, put on something simple, and being already up and dressed when her chambermaid entered, after thinking it over once more, and hesitating a short while, sent for porters,[21] left the house alone, and went to Henriette's.

Mademoiselle Duménil had just awakened when she was notified of a visit she was very far from expecting.

---

[20]That is, Madame Duménil, her sister-in-law—a substitution frequent in eighteenth-century language.

[21]She goes in a sedan chair (*chaise à porteurs*), instead of calling for a carriage.

"What are you doing here, Mademoiselle?" she cried out to Ernestine in surprise. "What business can be pressing enough to bring you here?"

"The most important of my life," Ernestine replied. "I have come to learn whether you are still that friend once so concerned for my plight, whose heart opened to my sufferings, and whose hand dried my tears! If you are unchanged, why did you distress and almost offend me yesterday? If you can no longer love me, tell me how I have lost your affection: I used to complain of being long neglected, unaccountably forgotten; shall I now complain of your injustice?" And putting her arms around her friend, pressing her tenderly to her, she said, "Speak, my dear Henriette, tell me *what separates us*, and why my happy situation seems to move you to pity."

"Your *happy situation!*" repeated Mademoiselle Duménil. "If you find it *happy*, can a faint reproach disrupt its bliss? But what design impels you to seek me out? Why urge me to speak? Did you not hear me?"

"No," said Ernestine. "For what are you reproaching me? What have I done? In what way do *our sentiments differ*? Does my conduct seem to you improper?" "This question astonishes me," replied Mademoiselle Duménil; and looking her in the eyes: "Dare you question me in that tranquil manner about such a shocking subject?" she asked. "Have you, forsaking your duties, also lost from memory the obligations they imposed upon you; have you no notion of them remaining? You blush," she added; "you lower your eyes: modesty[22] still shines on the noble and unassuming brow of Ernestine. Oh, how could she have banished it from her heart?"

"Your expressions, and not my faults, make me blush," said Ernestine. "I have exactly fulfilled the duties I have been taught to respect, and have nothing to be ashamed of. Yet you accuse me: I have *forgotten* these duties, I have *lost the very notion of them?* Who told you so; on what basis do you draw this judgment?"

"I would have never thought you capable of such surprising self-assurance," said Henriette. "But let us end this conversation; do not force me to explain the sentiments it may make me feel. Oh, Mademoiselle, you have made a perfectly willing, perfectly complete sacrifice to riches, if you have not even enough decency left to blush at the miserable station you have chosen!"

"Oh, God!" exclaimed Ernestine in tears, "is this a friend, is this Henriette who treats me so harshly? A *miserable* station! I have chosen *this station!* I have renounced *decency! Sacrificed it to riches!* I! How? When, on what

_____

[22]English has only the word "modesty" where French distinguishes between modesty in a general sense (*modestie*) and *pudeur*, which is sexual shame and timidity, used here because of Henriette's suppositions about Ernestine's liaison.

occasion? What, Mademoiselle, you dare to insult me so cruelly? You dare to impute crimes to me!"

Mademoiselle Duménil, moved by the tears of a young person long so dear to her heart, could not provoke her anguish without sharing it; her natural indulgence disposed her to excuse Ernestine, and put to her sister-in-law's account the waywardness of a simple girl so easily misguided. She reflected for a moment, then taking her friend's hand, said, "Be truthful; answer unhesitatingly what I ask. When I wrote to you from Brittany, why did you give me no news of yourself? How could you ignore my advice during my brother's illness? After his death I offered you a decent and agreeable refuge; why did you refuse it? And why, finally, was I instructed on your behalf not to bother myself further with your conduct?"

By responding to these questions, Ernestine revealed to Mademoiselle Duménil that she thought herself entitled to accuse her of neglect. Henriette saw that her friend had been led into a trap; she had no doubt that, in concert with the marquis de Clémengis, Madame Duménil had kept Ernestine from knowing anything of letters that might have enlightened her about the dangers of her situation. She sighed, and became more compassionate. "We have both been deceived," she said. "Because of two false-hearted creatures my foresight has been of no avail; they have basely taken advantage of the circumstances, of the fact that I was away, and of your credulity! But where does this sad assurance lead us? In your mind, you are happy! What chance is there of restoring you to your original principles? Having once tasted of opulence, is it easy to do without it? Could you give up the marquis de Clémengis, give up his self-serving favors; flee, despise, hate this vile man . . . ?" "Give him up! Flee him! Despise him!" Ernestine cried out. "What names you dare give him! And why should I flee him? What has he done? In what way does he deserve to provoke the horror you feel for him?"

"You embarrass me," replied Henriette. "How can my words occasion such surprise in you? Do you not receive this man's visits? Does he not spend part of the day in your rooms? Are others admitted there? Are you determined to continue this dishonorable relationship? If you love the marquis de Clémengis, if the very thought of leaving him is repugnant to you, makes you cry out in anguish, then what are you doing here? Tell me the reason for this strange proceeding: are you trying to excuse your conduct, to insist that I approve of it? What do you want from me; what are you asking of me? Why are you seeking me out?"

"A dishonorable relationship!" repeated Ernestine. "And since when does friendship dishonor the one who began it, inspires and shares it? No one is admitted to my rooms? Whoever would want to see me? The marquis de Clémengis is my only acquaintance, my sole friend. Raised far from society, accustomed to keeping myself busy, I have never yet felt the need to be entertained, to flee from myself, or the desire to form ties. Madame Duménil, formerly so sociable, left her friends behind once she recovered her property, and no longer had a thought . . ."

"Recovered her property!" interrupted Henriette. "What property can you mean?"

Then Ernestine related the story she had heard from Madame Duménil in the country, and failing to notice Henriette's surprise: "You reproach me for my affection for the marquis de Clémengis," she added; "if you knew him you would approve of it. Yes, the thought of never seeing him again is repugnant to me, it wounds my heart; a tender friendship has grown between us: it is all the happiness I have, and doubtless all of his as well! The presence of this amiable man inspires I know not what delightful sentiment, the charm of which is inexpressible: the moment he is near me, I feel happy; I read in his eyes that he too is happy, and I like to think that it is a single impulse that causes his pleasures and mine."

Henriette joined her hands together, and lifted her eyes toward heaven. "Dear God!" she cried, "have I rightly heard? What hope arises in my heart! This confession, her ingenuousness . . . Oh, my dear Ernestine, are you yet innocent?" In the sudden and tender transport of her joy, she pressed her charming friend to her breast. "No," she said, "no, Ernestine would never confess a shameful attachment with such openness: she is deceived, she is not seduced; there is still time, still time to save her from the danger to which her credulity exposes her."

Insistent questions and clear replies finally brought about the enlightenment that both desired. The marquis's conduct astonished Mademoiselle Duménil; it seemed exceptional to her, but she knew society too well to have a good opinion of it. What was Ernestine to think when she learned where this conduct could have led her: ah, yes, such tender attentions, such great favors, bestowed on her with such profusion and discretion, were designed to deprive her of something the loss of which could never be repaired by riches and grandeur.

Entering then into the details necessary to her purposes, Mademoiselle Duménil expounded on men's libertine and inconsistent way of thinking, on the notable contradiction between their principles and their morals. "Oh, my dear friend, you do not know them," she repeated. "They claim they were created to guide, sustain, protect a *timid, weak sex*: yet they alone attack it, encourage its timidity, and take advantage of its weakness; they have made unjust conventions among themselves to dominate women and subject them to their control; they have imposed duties upon them, laid down laws for them which, in a revoltingly bizarre manner, born of their own self-love, they urge them to break, and continually set traps for this *timid, weak sex* of which they dare consider themselves the counsel and support."

"Oh! Do not compare the marquis de Clémengis with those senseless men!" exclaimed Ernestine; "do not assume he had cruel intentions; never did he conceive the horrible plan of seducing me, of subjecting me to scorn and misery. No, his affection is as pure as mine. Ah! if only you could see him, speak to him . . ." "Well, then!" interrupted Mademoiselle Duménil, "I shall see him, I shall speak to him; I do hope his friendship is innocent and disinterested. But even assuming that, how can I excuse the imprudence of his conduct? By persuading you to live on an estate he had just purchased, did he not expose you to the appearance of living at his expense? When he concealed you from others' eyes, was he not leading them to believe that you existed for him alone? He hid his favors from you, but could he hide them from others? Is Madame Duménil unknown? Are people unaware of her means? Her former friends, surprised at no longer seeing her, have wished to learn the secret of her withdrawal; they have discovered it, bruited it about. Since the marquis's return, what notions can have arisen in the minds of your servants and his? Base notions, but malicious, elaborate ones, quickly transmitted. Did I myself not believe you were corrupted? Monsieur de Clémengis is your friend, you say? No, Ernestine, no, he is not; could the man who sacrifices your reputation to his amusement, to his pleasures, be a friend? Could he have a *pure affection*? But you weep," she continued, "you sigh, you lament; you are not listening to me."

"I have heard you only too well," said Ernestine. "You have just destroyed the peace of my soul, my whole life's happiness! Oh, why do you dispel such a flattering illusion?" And burying her face awash with tears in her friend's breast, she exclaimed, "My dear Henriette, forgive me; forgive my anguish, allow it to pour forth. I cannot applaud your reason; I cannot show gratitude for your goodness. Oh, did you have to enlighten me? My error made me so happy! How I hate society, its ways, its prejudices, its malicious observations! What do I owe this society in which I do not live? Indeed, must I sacrifice my happiness to its false opinions? Oh, what difference do its vain and presumptuous judgments make to me, when I am innocent, and my heart has nothing to be ashamed of?"

"You trouble, you distress me," replied Mademoiselle Duménil. "How attached you are to Monsieur de Clémengis! Is it only by piercing your heart with a thousand painful darts that I can restore you to yourself? But cease piercing my own heart with your cries, your laments that affect me too much. Why these tears? You are free, Ernestine; oh, good God, have I the right to force you, to wrest violently from you this happiness you regret losing so intensely? You can still enjoy it, nothing stands in the way of your desires. Forget you have seen me, banish the memory of my friendship, of my vain attempts; go, return to the vile, accommodating woman who has basely collaborated in providing you this passing felicity. It is not of me you should complain, but of her: that flighty woman is the true cause of your sufferings; may she not one day be the cause of your shame and remorse!"

"How miserable am I!" exclaimed Ernestine. "What turmoil and bitterness a moment has sown in my heart! That I should be thought subject to shame and remorse! Oh my dear Henriette, do not despise your friend; take no offense at my protests! I am weak, and maybe unjust; anguish oppresses my soul, casts down my spirits; I am not myself. Do not tell me to return to the woman who deceived me; I entrust myself to you, to your counsel, to your understanding, to your friendship! Oh, I have no regrets for the luxury in which I was living, or the fortune I am forsaking! But that amiable friend, so tender, so sincere, imprudent in your eyes but respectable in mine; that friend whose generous if always hidden hand showered me with gifts and asked nothing of me by way of return; that friend so dear, so worthy of my esteem, of my attachment, who took such pleasure in coming to see me, talking to me, being with me—must I grieve him, flee him, quit him cruelly, make him worry, cause him the same anguish I feel?"

"No, my dear Ernestine, you must not," replied Henriette. "On the contrary, you must see him, speak to him, get him to consent to your decision to leave Madame Duménil. Now, who said you should give up the enjoyment of an innocent comradeship, and force yourself to forgo the pleasure of receiving the visits of Monsieur de Clémengis? When you are no longer living off his favors, and have withdrawn to a decent refuge, you will have every freedom and right to cultivate this friendship so dear to your heart. Write to the marquis, and invite him to come here instantly: you will avert the worry you fear will overtake him. A minute's conversation will reveal to me what he has in mind. He will not disapprove of my counsel, I hope; but if he does, will you not be free to follow his?"

Ernestine picked up a pen, and with trembling hand traced these words:

> I have just learned that I owe neither respect nor gratitude to Madame Duménil. Do not look for me at her house; I am leaving her permanently. Are you, you who for a year have enjoyed my friendship and esteem, false-hearted? If you can justify your intentions in the eyes of a respectable maiden, come to the house of Mademoiselle Duménil, where I await you fearfully, impatiently. I desire, I hope, I believe you are worthy of my sentiments: oh, come

prove it to my friend—to my only friend if you have deceived me!

Monsieur de Clémengis had just arrived from Versailles and was intending to go to Ernestine's, when Mademoiselle Duménil's servant brought him this note. He complied without hesitation, and soon stood before Henriette, with that noble assurance that comes from the certainty of never having violated the laws of honor.

When he entered, he seemed surprised to find her alone. Ernestine had just slipped into a study from where she could hear him: experiencing for the first time at the marquis's arrival an emotion without hint of pleasure, she feared his presence, and felt the desire to hide from him the impulses of her heart.

Casting her eyes on Monsieur de Clémengis, Mademoiselle Duménil became even more indulgent for her friend's tender weakness. How would such a charming face not have made the most vivid impression on a person so young, so unguarded against passion, so accustomed to following nothing but her heart's inspirations? Henriette admired the marquis, and hoped a good natural disposition corresponded to this amiable exterior. "Will you forgive me, Monsieur," she said, "for entering thus into confidential matters, and seeking to discover your secrets; for daring to call you to account for conduct the apparent irregularity of which is doubtless justified by the hidden motive of your actions? Will you refuse to tell me your designs on Ernestine?"

"In truth, Mademoiselle, I have none," said the marquis; "and you have no idea how you embarrass me with a question I have asked myself a thousand times, without being able to give myself a satisfactory answer. I desire Ernestine's tranquillity, her happiness; I have arranged for means of making her happy; my heart has admitted to itself these intentions, but I am aware of no others. Dare I in turn, Mademoiselle, ask you what you find untoward about my actions and why you seem to find fault with my conduct?"

"I am sorry, Monsieur, very sorry," replied Henriette, "that you can believe yourself above reproach when you risk the reputation of a young person who has nothing but her virtue. Did you have the right to take her from my sight, deprive her of my counsel, bring her to renounce such a simple but peaceful station in order to taste the pleasures of a passing opulence, accustom her to enjoying it, and perhaps induce her to acquire it through the sacrifice of her moral honesty? Well then, Monsieur, do you reproach yourself for nothing, when it has pleased you to kindle in her a passion that places her in the cruel necessity of living in corruption or misery?"

"I am vulnerable to this last reproach," replied the marquis; "I deserve it, and often make it to myself. Given

Ernestine's position, given mine, I should neither have indulged my inclination, nor excited in her a passion that could be fulfilled only if one of us made too great a sacrifice to the other. But did I attempt to seduce her? Did I deceive her with dazzling promises? Did I give her false expectations? Did I abuse her credulity? Did I even stir her heart with words of passion? Did I so much as allow myself to express my feelings? Content with the pleasure of loving, charmed by the sweetness of finding favor, I enjoyed a happiness unknown, perhaps, to ordinary men. Ernestine shared it! Oh, Mademoiselle, what you are taking from both of us with the terrible enlightenment you have just given her!"

Mademoiselle Duménil, somewhat embarrassed by this sort of reproach, did not wish to let Monsieur de Clémengis think it was indiscreet or officious zeal that had impelled her to get to the bottom of an intrigue in which he was involved[23]; she told him how they had chanced to meet the day before, and hid from him nothing of what had just transpired between her and Ernestine.

"I am willing to let you in on all my secrets, Mademoiselle," the marquis resumed; "I do not contest your rights over a young person whom you have protected for many years. By rescuing her from a worse than mediocre sta-

---

[23]The question of rank is pertinent here: that is, a woman of the bourgeoisie has presumed to pry into the affairs of a nobleman.

tion, I wished to do for modest and helpless beauty what my peers do daily in the interest of baseness, vice, and scandal. Your friend is not enjoying a *passing opulence*: she is rich, free, and independent. Having been favored all winter by unremitting good fortune, and forced my luck without seeing it run out,[24] I found myself before leaving for Italy in possession of a considerable sum; nothing prevented my disposing of it as I wished, and I decided to use it to change the fate of your brother's amiable pupil. My design was to put it in your hands, but your departure forced me to take other measures. Following the advice of Madame Duménil, I deposited a portion of Ernestine's fortune with the public accountant with whom you yourself, Mademoiselle, had invested her earlier capital: the estate where she was living belongs to her, it was bought in her name and through the services of that honest man. If I have concealed my own services from your young friend, it was out of a sentiment for which you cannot blame me. Now you know all: judge me, Mademoiselle, and pray tell me whether my mysterious conduct seems to you criminal, and whether I have deserved to have Ernestine ask of me: *Are you false-hearted?*"

Henriette reflected for a minute. The marquis de Clémengis's noble candor, his generosity, such tender, disinterested love, seemed a new sentiment to her, of which

---

[24]That is, he had been pressing his luck at gambling and always won.

the elevated society in which she had lived since her child-
hood had never given her any notion. She began to look
upon Ernestine's friend with a sort of veneration. But still
seeking to be sure she was making no mistake, she asked,
"Would you consent, Monsieur, to allowing Ernestine to
enjoy your gifts in the convent where I intend to escort
her this evening?"

"Oh, let her enjoy them wherever they will make her
happy!" exclaimed Monsieur de Clémengis. "Did I oblige
her in order to constrain her? No, Mademoiselle, no, I repeat, she is free, she is independent, and I would hold myself in contempt if I dared presume any rights over her."

Mademoiselle Duménil arose impetuously, hurried to
her study, took Ernestine by the hand, and led her into
the presence of Monsieur de Clémengis. "Give thanks to
your amiable, your generous protector," she said to her.
"You have no need to blush at his favors, you have nothing to fear from them; perhaps you were not born to
accept such things, but the gifts of friendship are never
degrading. Strive to deserve through active and constant
gratitude the friend your happy fate provides you."

Ernestine had heard everything. Moved by a tender sentiment to which she dared not allow full reign, her heart's
only expression for some while was her tears. "Mademoiselle Duménil anticipates by a few days," the marquis said
to her, "a proposition I was preparing to make to you.

48

Madame Duménil's continual complaints, her insistence on introducing you to society, were going to force me to beg you to leave her; your friend spares me an explanation I was finding difficult; I dreaded the moment when I should speak to you, and still more the consequences of an enlightenment I hesitated to give you. But why do you weep?" he asked her tenderly. "Might you have some aversion to the refuge we are proposing for you?"

"Oh! Monsieur," said Ernestine, "could I fail to be content with the refuge you elect for me? I shall follow Mademoiselle's advice, I shall submit to the laws you see fit to lay down for me; they will be forever my life's rule."[25] "I, lay down laws for you, my dear Ernestine!" exclaimed the marquis. "What language! Can I hear it without anguish?" And turning to Henriette: "And I beg of you, Mademoiselle," he said in a tender, even sad voice, "and I beg you to persuade your friend to treat me more kindly."

Ernestine extended her hand to him, and was about to speak; but her fear lest she be seeing the marquis for the last time weighed on her heart and tied her tongue. A few words punctuated with sighs revealed to Monsieur de Clémengis what was on her mind. He was moved, touched by it; he took her hand, pressed it gently, kissed it. "We shall not be separated," he told her. "I shall visit

---

[25]Ernestine's choice of word (*règle*) is a sign of deference, since it normally refers to the set of rules governing a given monastic order.

you often; you will always be dear to me, you will be constantly in my thoughts. Dry your tears, lift your charming eyes upon two persons by whom you are so truly loved; do me the pleasure of congratulating me in your friend's eyes for having never obliged you to lower yours in her presence for any concession I have made to my desires."

Mademoiselle Duménil joined with the marquis to console Ernestine; together they took every measure that could make this amiable girl's new situation both agreeable and peaceful. Ernestine herself chose the abbey of Montmartre, and asked to retire there.[26] The marquis promised he would promptly dispatch thither her chambermaid, the only domestic she wished to keep, and relieved her of the burden of notifying Madame Duménil of such an abrupt separation. At his request, Henriette consented to receive Ernestine's most precious possessions into her house, whence they would be transported to the abbey. She accepted responsibility for the oversight of her friend's property, and the marquis's offer to deposit its titles in her hands.

While going along with these arrangements, which were to cost him his freedom to see Ernestine at any hour

---

[26]Montmartre was then an independent town north of Paris, to which it was annexed in 1860. Since the Middle Ages there had been a number of religious establishments there. It is apparent that Ernestine has no intention of taking vows; at the time many convents had apartments that women could rent for personal retreat (as does the Princesse de Clèves at the end of her story).

of the day, Monsieur de Clémengis made an effort to appear tranquil; but as he was unaccustomed to disguising his soul's impulses, his glances revealed the turmoil and disarray of a restless passion. He took Ernestine's hands, and looking at her with indescribable affection, "Oh, my charming friend," he said, "never forget a man who was able to spend so many hours in your company, and repress an ardor the object and intensity of which offered such a natural excuse. I love you! You did not know this; it is sweet to me to tell you, to repeat it to you! Yes, I love you, I adore you! What an effort it required of me to keep silent about it for so long! I congratulate myself for respecting you: the greater my desires, and the more the innocence and sensibility of your heart offered me the flattering thought of an assured triumph, the more satisfying is the victory I have won over myself. If you think you owe some return for my tender, my solid friendship, grant me the reward of such a difficult exertion, of such constant restraint: cease to grieve, banish this cruel sadness that overcomes you; let me see no more trace of it in these dear eyes. Ah, you know well that my whole happiness depends upon being sure of Ernestine's!"

The marquis then took leave of Mademoiselle Duménil without waiting for her reply; he started to go, then returned to her, and asked her in a timid voice whether he might be allowed to see her again. Henriette, gentle, affectionate, virtuous without abrasiveness, scorned the kind of often affected and always repellent severity that makes propriety more inconvenient than respectable; she did not believe she should deprive the marquis of seeing Ernestine: she replied to him cheerfully that she would be happy to receive his visits.

Obliged to go downstairs at dinner time, Henriette did not insist that Ernestine appear in front of her cousin. When she came back up, she was told that her friend had been unable to bring herself to eat anything: she found her downcast, bathed in tears, her head drooping on her breast, her face half hidden under a handkerchief drenched with tears. "Now, what causes this renewed anguish?" exclaimed Henriette. "What reason, what thoughts wring from you these bitter tears?"

"I don't know," Ernestine replied; "I can't tell why my soul is so cruelly oppressed. I felt no desires, I conceived no expectations, my felicity seemed supreme happiness to me: it filled my heart completely, it never allowed me to formulate hopes; never did I glimpse in the future something better than what I was then enjoying. And yet, my dear Henriette, I feel that I have lost something precious; I have just been robbed, deprived of . . . of what? Not even wishes! Oh, what sad illumination the marquis's words have brought into my mind! *Ernestine's position, my own, do not allow us to be happy, unless one of us makes too great a sacrifice to the other!"* She paused, she sighed, turned away her eyes, for fear of encountering Henriette's. "Dear Clémengis!" she said, "thou shalt not make *too great a sacrifice* so as to make Ernestine happy! She does not require that; she does not desire a happiness that would taint thy glory. My eyes are open, I see all that separates us; but why, but how is it, that one experiences such intense anguish in renouncing a hope one did not have?"

Mademoiselle Duménil's caresses, the marquis's visits, time, and reason dissipated Ernestine's sorrow to some extent; but a mild melancholy became her habitual humor.[27] After spending a month at Henriette's, she went to the convent. They had prepared a comfortable and pleasant apartment for her, throughout which she discovered marks of her lover's attentions: a small library made up of books chosen by the marquis provided her a useful distraction and the means of acquiring knowledge. She continued to take music lessons, busied herself with reading, and did not neglect a talent that had become precious to her through the pleasure it gave her of multiplying the image of Monsieur de Clémengis, whose cherished features reappeared in every subject that came to her imagination, and her studio filled with her lover's portraits.

---

[27]Melancholy was still thought of in terms of its physical cause, which was black bile.

Mademoiselle Duménil visited her often. The marquis sometimes accompanied her, but he rarely allowed himself to go to the abbey alone. From the very moment he decided to place Ernestine under Henriette's tutelage, he had striven to combat his passion; according to his principles, he could not make her happy without the risk of overturning his fortune, of failing in the respect due his uncle, and also to a great family whose alliance his uncle had in view for him.[28] The old and important case on which his expectations depended was just then being examined, and the judgment concerning it was still uncertain; if Monsieur de Clémengis were to lose all at once his suit and his uncle's protection, and be forced to leave the service,[29] give up the court, and live far from society, could he be sure that his desires, after his possession of Ernestine, would not diminish, that the constancy of his sentiments would render his pleasures durable, that the joys of his marriage would efface the bitter memory of the sacrifices he had made to love? Who could assure him he would continue to think as he did now? Perhaps one day, his regrets making him unfair, he would cease to love the innocent cause of his penury; perhaps he would dare

---

[28]This explains the "sacrifice" to which Clémengis referred in his own case: his rank, but also his obligations to his lineage. It is also the first allusion to a prospective marriage.

[29]Not because of dishonor but for lack of funds: an officer was not paid; on the contrary, he furnished his own equipment and provided for his own sustenance.

blame her for his own imprudence, make her bear the bitterness of his sorrows, make her miserable, and deprive her forever of that peace and happiness that he himself had wished to secure for her.

These reflections confirmed him in the resolution to resist his love, to deny himself the attentions to her that fostered it. He tested his strength, forced himself with great difficulty to go several days without seeing Ernestine or writing to her; but soon reproaching himself for this apparent neglect, he hastened to her, drank in the pleasure of looking at her; and finding her sad and downcast, he accused himself of cruelty, asked himself how he could have grieved her, how he could have given rise to a movement of anguish in that affectionate soul.

The tender girl dared not complain of him; she had become timid, blushed at her turmoil and did her best to hide it; but her languishing looks, her sighs, her anxious questions, revealed the fear of being no longer loved. Losing sight of all his plans, the marquis thought only of reassuring her; he gave in to the joy of expressing his sentiments to her; and bringing back to her mind the time when, free to converse, they spent such delightful hours together, he seemed to reproach her for having sought enlightenment that was superfluous to her happiness. "Oh, why," he would say to her, "have you learned to fear me, and to distrust yourself?"

Touched by such words, moved by her own thoughts, Ernestine held her peace, wept, and longed perhaps for her former simplicity. Three months went by that brought no change in her situation. When spring returned, the marquis prepared to leave her to rejoin his regiment. Both of them were much affected by the approaching separation. Their farewells were long and tender, they both wept, and far from exhorting each other to love less, they repeated a thousand times over that they would love each other forever.

A short while after Monsieur de Clémengis's departure, Ernestine began to weary of her retreat; she desired to go to the country, to see once more that agreeable lodging that was a present from her lover, prepared and enhanced at his behest. Henriette cautioned her that she ought not live there alone. This obstacle, which vexed Ernestine, was lifted by chance: a matter in which her heart engaged her caused her to find a companion.

Madame de Ranci, age thirty-six, still fair, amiable, and unhappy, who had retired three years earlier to the abbey, had consistently shown goodwill and friendship to the young Ernestine. A widow, reduced by untimely misfortunes to the barest necessities, she had nothing left but a small annuity, which was dependent on an individual who through bad luck or misconduct disarranged his finances;

pressed by his creditors, he fled to Holland, and abandoned Madame de Ranci to all the horrors of dire poverty.

Ernestine, raised, maintained, enriched by the tender compassion of her friends, took pleasure in bestowing her liberality on all those who made her remember her original station; her heart, always receptive to the cries of the indigent, sought to render to humanity the succor she herself had received from it.

Deeply affected by Madame de Ranci's adversity, she took measures with Mademoiselle Duménil to transfer to the name of that bereft woman the small inheritance from Madame Dufresnoi, and added enough to it to replace her loss and even increase her revenue somewhat. Gratitude compounding friendship in the heart of an honest and affectionate woman, Madame de Ranci soon felt for Ernestine the sentiments of a tender mother, and joyfully accepted the proposition to share her life, to live with her always and accompany her to her country estate, to which they repaired a month after Monsieur de Clémengis's departure.

Ernestine was ecstatic to see once more these premises that were dear to her heart. She did not disguise from Madame de Ranci the cause of the pleasure she felt living there; she showed her the marquis's letters, her replies, talked about her sentiments for that amiable man; told her about her obligations, her gratitude, her affection, the sweetness she experienced in thinking about him; and when her friend asked her where such an intense love was to lead her, when she inquired into her expectations, sighs and tears interrupted the effusions of the heart: she admitted that she had none. Without rejecting Madame de Ranci's prudent counsel, or being put off by her reflections, she listened to her, conceded the appropriateness of her observations, and made it apparent that they failed to persuade her; nothing could induce her to forget the marquis, to give up the pleasure of loving him and the assurance of his affection.

Toward summer's end, Mademoiselle Duménil, about to return to Brittany, decided before her departure to spend a few days with Ernestine. While taking leave of her, she enjoined her not to await Monsieur de Clémengis in that splendid isolation, and did not leave until she obtained from her a promise to return soon to the convent.

This word given to Mademoiselle Duménil soon posed a dilemma for the amiable and tender Ernestine. The marquis would be coming back; he implored her to remain at home, to spend the fall in the country, and allow him to see her once more with a freedom she had no reason to fear he would abuse; Madame de Ranci's presence was sufficient, he insisted, to protect her from malicious commentary. The same plea was renewed in each of his letters;

he pressed her so urgently it was as if his entire happiness depended on obtaining from her this concession.

The helpless Ernestine could not but grant a favor so insistently solicited. "I owe him everything," she would say to Madame de Ranci; "shall I do nothing for him? To resist his desires is to accuse myself of ingratitude: is it my place to grieve him? Indeed, why should I not yield to his wishes in everything honor does not forbid? Why should I sacrifice to the fear of being unjustly suspected the genuine pleasure of giving him joy? You will strengthen me against myself, you will be so good as to fulfill in my behalf the role of tender and vigilant mother, you will not leave my side; a witness to my conduct, you will exonerate me to Henriette; and what difference does anyone else make? The esteem of my friends, and my own, are enough for my tranquillity." In vain did Madame de Ranci oppose so determined a resolution, and Monsieur de Clémengis had the pleasure of joining Ernestine in the country, and being assured that he owed this indulgence to love.

He savored it for several days, not appearing to imagine anything beyond the happiness he had anticipated; but can a confessed love ever contain itself within the strict bounds prescribed by friendship? A desire satisfied gives rise to another yet more ardent; wishes multiply, hopes go further, a concession received opens the heart to the expectation of a greater one; the immense spaces that seemed to distance a barely visible point imperceptibly disappear, and thought fixes upon the object one dared not even glimpse.

Though free to prolong his visits, to spend a part of the day with Ernestine, the marquis de Clémengis expressed irritation. Madame de Ranci's continual presence did not suit him, and her scruple never to leave her young friend's side made her seem to him unbearable. "Did you have to accustom that woman to following you about so conspicuously," he said to Ernestine, "never to lose sight of you? Do you require of her this importunate persistence? Do you fear me? Have you lost your esteem for me? What, precautions against me? Is it you, is it Ernestine who shows me an offensive mistrust? What coldness! what reserve! No, your friendship is no longer as tender; oh, what has become of that time, that happy time, in this same place, when you rushed to meet me with such intense joy, when your arm leaned upon mine,[30] when we explored together every path in this wood you so enjoyed! Oh, my dear friend, have you then so greatly changed?"

These reproaches moved Ernestine, filled her heart, provoked her tears, but never the slightest complaint; she bore with resignation the dismaying sameness of these conversations. The marquis's grief, his pallor, his dejec-

---

[30]By custom, a gentleman offered his arm to escort a lady; she could then express her sentiments by pressing against it.

tion, raised fears in her soul; she trembled for a life so precious. "I shall not be badgering you for long," he would say, his eyes filling with tears. She began to regret an indulgence of which she had not foreseen the consequences. "My imprudence now has rekindled a passion long repressed," she repeated to Madame de Ranci; "so far I knew only its sweetness; now I experience all its bitterness." This woman, alarmed at the danger to her youthful friend, urged her to return to Montmartre. Ernestine agreed to do so; but before her departure she wrote to Monsieur de Clémengis, and sent her letter to him by express at the very moment she entered the convent. He opened it eagerly, and great was his surprise when he found these words:

Letter from Ernestine

What anguish for me, Monsieur, to provoke your complaints, to blame myself for all you suffer, and reproach myself for the terrible condition you are in! Can it really be I who grieve you? Can I believe this, can I be quite sure of it, when your happiness is the object, the sole object of my heart's every wish? Alas, by what fate does that happiness seem now to depend on the misconduct of a girl you used to respect? Be judge of your own cause, of mine, and pronounce between your heart and mine.

You are hurt by my reserve? But, Monsieur, is it permissible for me to treat you with a familiarity that was once excusable thanks to my ignorance? For a long time I dared to look upon you as a dear brother: I was not struck by the extreme disparity between our fortunes; in those happy times nothing prevented tokens of my innocent affection. Nothing in me is changed; oh, why do you insist on thinking it is? It is not you, Monsieur, it is myself that I fear. I am young, I owe you everything. I love you; yes, Monsieur, I love you, I say it, I repeat it with pleasure; I am not ashamed to love you. The first moment you appeared to my sight brought forth this affection, which time has made so intense: a sentiment dear to my heart, the only one that makes me want to live. So many favors, so generously showered on me, assured me a peaceful future, but the love you inspired in me constituted my happiness, my ultimate happiness! To think constantly about you, to work at preserving your friendship, to deserve my respectable friend's esteem; to see you occasionally, to read in your eyes that my presence brought you joy: that for me was the supreme good! Is such felicity destroyed forever? Will you not restore it to me? Nay, it is no longer in your power to restore it!

You shall not be badgering me for long! How cruel is this expression! I cannot bear the certainty of making you unhappy; it pierces my soul and rends my heart. By withdrawing, and forsaking the place where I saw you without constraint, I have followed prudent counsel; but I am not fleeing you, it is not my intention to raise a barrier between you and me. Prepared to leave this refuge if you wish, I submit my action to your decision. If, to save your life, I must become despicable, renounce my principles, my own esteem and perhaps yours, I do not hesitate between an interest so dear and my personal interest. You may dispose, Monsieur, of the fate of a girl prepared, determined to give up everything for your happiness; but before accepting such a great sacrifice, allow me to remit into your hands all the gifts you have made to me. To keep them, to make use of them, would be to let you believe you have enriched me for my undoing: let us save your honor at least, and a small portion of mine; may it never be said that I was base enough to accept a price for my innocence. On those conditions, Monsieur, the tender, unhappy Ernestine will do whatever your reply shall prescribe to her.

"Good God!" exclaimed the marquis as he finished reading, "have I driven this charming girl to write such things to me? What a strange proposal! But what goodness, what affection, what generosity in this abandonment of her principles, of her very self! Amiable Ernestine! Would I—I—defile thee? Would I abuse thy love, thy noble confidence . . . ? Oh! thou hast nothing to fear from thy lover, thy friend, thy grateful friend. May he perish, the unjust, cruel man who would presume to found his happiness on the submission of a sweet, affectionate creature, capable of effacing herself to make him happy!"

Monsieur de Clémengis hastened to reply to the anxious Ernestine. The agitation in his mind, the emotion in his heart, did not permit him to put much order into his letter. He thanked her for such extraordinary proof of her sentiments; he complained of it also, reproaching her gently for suspecting him of a design he was not contriving. "Oh, how could you have believed," he said to her, "that your friend could wish to be your despot?" He ended his letter with sad, vague phrases that seemed to indicate he would come to see her that evening; he promised to reveal something to her that would explain what he dared not say then, and was unhappy, most unhappy to have to tell her.

Ernestine was with Madame de Ranci when the letter from Monsieur de Clémengis was brought to her. She took it with trembling hand, and held it for a long time without daring to open it; a deathly pallor spread across her face. "Here is the decree of my fate," she said. "Oh, Madame de Ranci, if you knew . . . ! What have I done? What does he say? I am undone!"

This woman, unaware of the subject of her terror, was astonished at the consternation in which she saw her. Ernestine finally broke the seal, and as she lifted her timid eyes on that dear hand, tears of joy soon flooded that consoling letter; she pressed it to her heart, kissed it a thousand times. "Oh, my respectable friend! Forgive me," she repeated. "No, I ought not to have doubted thee." Then, revealing to Madame de Ranci the cause of her terror, she shared with her friend's soul a portion of the emotions that were affecting hers.

As she reread the marquis's letter, Ernestine began again to worry. "Oh! what then is he to tell me?" she asked Madame de Ranci. "Maybe he intends to leave me, give up seeing me; everything suggests a sad separation. What do these phrases mean: *When I said to you, 'I shall stop badgering you,' I was far from wishing to arouse in your mind these ominous thoughts that I see too well have obsessed it. I have sought, I have avoided the opportunity to reveal to you the meaning of these words. Alas, my dear Ernestine! What a sad confession I have for you! What a sacrifice my duty requires! I no longer am allowed to live for myself; I no longer am allowed to hope for happiness.* Oh! I am going to lose him," she cried. "My heart tells me! But how is it he cannot live happily, and see me, and love me? How can the same sentiment produce such diverse effects? My love is such a great happiness for me! Must his own disrupt his life's satisfactions?"

She awaited impatiently the hour when she thought Monsieur de Clémengis would come to visit. The time went by more slowly than she wished; night fell, and her anxiety increased. The next day, upon awakening, she was presented with a letter from the marquis. She hastily tore open the envelope, and avidly seeking the confirmation of her fears, found it in these words:

Letter from Monsieur de Clémengis

Oh, my dear Ernestine! After the touching proof you have just given me of your sentiments, can I, without expiring of anguish, announce to you my departure and the event that is to follow it? Must I leave you, bid you an eternal farewell? Must I pierce your heart with the same dagger that is rending mine?

Amiable girl! Born for my life's happiness, worthy of the most brilliant future: oh, if only mine lay in my own power! Duty, gratitude, engagements long since entered into, overturn all my expectations. But had I any? How did I flatter myself . . . ? Oh, should I have led you to share a futile passion? What bitterness, what regrets mix with such terrible anguish! Will you forgive me? Will you not despise me? Will you ever hate me? My dear, my tender friend, pray reassure me about these fears, tell me you forgive me; do not refuse me a consolation my heart, my grieving heart, so requires.

My life's unhappiness is finally settled. My uncle has lifted all the obstacles that had deferred my marriage; he constrains me, he forces me to go pay suit to Mademoiselle de Saint-André. In an hour I depart with her father; he is taking me to an estate where the maréchale[31] de Saint-André awaits us. Her daughter leaves the convent tomorrow; we shall be introduced to each other, and shall soon be united, without being consulted, with no concern over whether our hearts are disposed to give of themselves. Can it be, dear Ernestine, that I am about to bind myself—forever! And it is not to you . . .

I had expected to enjoy my freedom longer. We were to await the decision of the parlement.[32] The uncertainty of my claim to a rich inheritance, to huge back payments, postponed the consent of the

---

[31]Wife of the maréchal (marshall). Maréchal is one of the highest military ranks and also a noble title. There had been a real maréchal de Saint-André in the sixteenth century, whose affiliation with the duc de Guise and the connétable (constable) de Montmorency is mentioned in Lafayette's *La Princesse de Clèves*.

[32]A supreme court in the province in question.

maréchal de Saint-André. My uncle's largesse now confounds me: a donation[33] assures me of all his property, and I have no hope remaining.

Shall I entreat you to forget me? No, oh no, I cannot wish to be forgotten by you, I cannot desire to forget you: you shall always be present in my thoughts, always dear to my heart. I shall think of you constantly; I shall write to you, tell you about my esteem, my friendship, and despite myself, perhaps, about my affection. It is not to urge you to share it still that I shall recall it, but to prove to you that time can neither lessen nor extinguish it.

Live in peace, live in happiness; may the memory of a sincere, genuine, constant friend occasionally bring a sigh; but let that sigh be tender and not painful . . . I cannot hold back my tears; they flow from my eyes, blotting out what I write. Oh, my generous friend! You will doubtless shed some too; may they be less bitter than mine! I love you, I adore you, I flee you, I am losing you, I am the most unfortunate of men.

What emotions this reading stirred in the heart of the affectionate Ernestine! A hundred times she interrupted it to give free vent to her tears, her sighs, her laments. "He is leaving," she said, "he is fleeing from me; I shall not see him again! He is to be joined with the happy wife chosen for him. He tells me to live in *peace and happiness*: oh, how could I be at peace far from him, happy without him?" She spent the entire day grieving and complaining

---

[33]*Donation entre vivants*: a legal document transferring property directly rather than as a legacy following the uncle's death.

of the marquis. "What hardness!" she would exclaim. "Could he leave without seeing me, without speaking to me, without mingling his tears with mine?" She wept; she wrote; tore up the letters she had begun, plunged into the depths of anguish; once more picked up her pen, and set it down again. Her agitation and the violence of her transports finally left her exhausted; she was ill, dejected, languishing for several days. But the marquis's letters, Madame de Ranci's exhortations, Mademoiselle Duménil's return, her care, her friendship, restored to her soul a semblance of calm. She got in the habit of saying to herself and repeating that she had never hoped for anything; she ceased to complain of her fate, resolved to submit to it, and sought in reason the strength to bear her suffering with resignation.

Two months went by, during which the marquis de Clémengis wrote regularly to his amiable friend. He did not tell her whether the knot had been tied; she dared not ask, fearing to find out; but she was soon to be enlightened about what had happened to Monsieur de Clémengis, and a sad experience would teach her what anguish one incurs in the course of these too-tender attachments to which the heart abandons itself with such pleasure, seeing in them the source of such intense and constant happiness.

One of Mademoiselle Duménil's relatives was to be wed in the country, about ten leagues from Paris. She was marrying a very wealthy man; as he had long looked forward to the happy day when she would be his, this lover, in the fullness of his joy, wanted a splendid wedding and prepared a festive celebration. Henriette, invited to share in the pleasures everyone expected to enjoy in places devoted to entertainment, prevailed upon Ernestine's indulgence to accompany her on this short, agreeable journey. Ernestine was reluctant, but finally yielded to her friend's insistence. Before leaving, she enjoined Madame de Ranci to send to her by express any letters that came; but several days went by before Ernestine received any news of either her or the marquis.

It had not occurred to Mademoiselle Duménil, in taking her friend to the country, that of all diversions the least likely to distract her was the spectacle she was being asked to witness. "They are perhaps holding the same festivities at the maréchal de Saint-André's," said Ernestine with a sigh; "but the marquis's heart is not filled with such sweet joy; he is not in love, he does not enjoy the pleasures in which these happy lovers are indulging. Yet he is not writing to me! Do you believe," she asked Henriette, "he has stopped writing to me? Will he deprive me of my only remaining consolation? Oh, doubtless he will deprive me of it! He will no longer think of me, will no longer even inquire whether I still exist. Never mind, he will still be dear to me; my sentiments for him will constantly fill my thoughts; never, never will I lose sight of the marquis de Clémengis; and if time at length allows me to think of him without anguish, I am very sure I will never think of him without interest." Henriette attempted to assuage her sorrows, to calm her anxieties; but Ernestine's situation was about to become so trying that the counsel and care of friendship could do nothing to help her heart.

Monsieur de Maugis, a friend of the hosts, arrived the morning everyone was preparing to return to Paris. He was chided for failing to heed insistent invitations, and reminded of his promise. He replied that the event about which they must have learned was a sufficient excuse. As everyone then gathered around him, ten persons questioned him at once. "How is this!" he said with surprise. "You have not heard about the comte de Saint-Servains's misfortune, about my brother's, and the marquis de Clémengis's exile?"[34]

Ernestine was entering the salon. These words froze her; she remained standing by the doorway, steadied herself against a panel, and summoned all the strength left her by this blow to her heart in order to listen to Monsieur de Maugis.

---

[34]The comte de Saint-Servains is evidently the uncle to whom Clémengis has alluded before but without naming him. Exile means not expatriation but orders to remain at a certain distance from the court: he will be banished to his estate, Clémengis.

"Indeed," he continued, "the comte de Saint-Servains is closely guarded, his papers have been seized, his effects confiscated. Since my brother was in his confidence, he has been placed under guard: an impenetrable silence prevents our learning the crime imputed to them. Envy has blackened a man whose genius and application made his administration so successful, whose integrity is known, whose congeniality won every heart: may he confound calumny, and live to see his vile accusers at his feet!"

"How I pity your brother," then said the chevalier d'Elmont. "How I pity the amiable Marquis de Clémengis! He was to marry Mademoiselle de Saint-André; now there will be no marriage." "No, assuredly not," replied Monsieur de Maugis. "He received this devastating news and the order to go to Clémengis two hours before the signing of the articles,[35] and made haste to notify the maréchal, himself breaking off their mutual engagements."

"Oh my Lord," added the chevalier d'Elmont, "a most cruel circumstance makes of his uncle's disgrace a double misfortune for him: was his suit not being adjudicated at just this time?" "True," replied Monsieur de Maugis, "and everyone in Paris thinks he will lose it."

As these words were spoken, Henriette came up quietly to Ernestine, and putting one arm around her and

---

[35]That is, the marriage contract.

escorting her out of the salon, she helped her walk and guided her to her room.

Wan, cold, lifeless, Ernestine seemed insensitive to this terrible and unforeseen news; she looked about her with vacant eyes, unable to speak or breathe. In vain did Mademoiselle Duménil urge her to shed tears as she bathed her in her own; Ernestine's heavy heart did not allow her to weep. Finally looking into her friend's eyes, she stared at her for a long while, and said, lifting her feeble and trembling hands heavenward: "Would I were dead; oh, why am I not dead, rather than learn that Monsieur de Clémengis is unhappy!"

Her tears, now flowing abundantly, relieved somewhat the oppression of her soul and revived her; but what agitation, what cries of anguish followed on her dejection! "Exiled, ruined, undone!" she repeated. "He, the marquis de Clémengis!"

Suddenly appearing to calm down, she wiped her tears, took Henriette's hands, and looking at her for a moment, lowering her eyes, raising them to her again, sighing deeply, she appeared hesitant to reveal her intentions to her.

"I grieve you," she said; "alas, I am going perhaps to horrify you; but in the name of our friendship, do not object to what I have in mind. I have a plan: do not oppose it by any reason, by any argument. Oh, my dear Henriette! I will not abandon Monsieur de Clémengis. He is exiled, his marriage is broken off, his fortune destroyed; he is going to lose the rest of his expectations![36] He is distressed, miserable! I mean to leave, and go find him: seeing me will perhaps mitigate his sufferings; if I cannot console him, I shall share his woes; I mean to grieve, suffer, die with him! Don't say a thing, no, don't say a thing; don't talk to me either about society, or about its cruel proprieties; I reject them if hardness accompanies them. Are there laws more holy than those of friendship? Duties more sacred than those of gratitude? To whom am I beholden? I have no family: if what I do is a fault, I alone will bear its shame. I mean to liquidate everything I own; I mean to restore secretly to Monsieur de Clémengis all the property I have received from him. For how could I enjoy it now? Happy in others' eyes, ungrateful in my own, how could I bear to live?"

Mademoiselle Duménil thought too nobly not to approve a part of her friend's design; and in that part that seemed to her to require further reflection, she saw her so riveted to her own intentions that to undertake to dissuade her from going to Clémengis would have much distressed her, without any assurance she could change her resolution: therefore she said nothing, leaving it to

---

[36]Ernestine means the family wealth he hoped to recover from the lawsuit, which he now presumably will lose.

Ernestine to interpret her silence, and both of them hastened back to Paris.

Along the way, Ernestine remembered an honest old man who looked after the business of Monsieur de Clémengis and was extremely devoted to him; his name was Lefranc. She had often seen him with Monsieur Duménil, when she had lived in his house. The marquis had hired the painter at the recommendation of Monsieur Lefranc, who was forever vaunting his talent. She remembered that Lefranc lived in the vicinity, and her first thought when she arrived in Montmartre, where she decided to spend the night, was to send this man a message urging him to come see her early the next morning: an important matter in which he could oblige her required her, she told him, to speak with and consult him. He came to the abbey at the appointed time.

The presence of a man who loved Monsieur de Clémengis and who cared for him stirred the most intense emotion in Ernestine's heart. She tried to explain herself, and began to speak, but her tears forced her to stop.

The good man, charmed to see his former friend's fair pupil again, assured her of his eagerness to serve her, and protested a thousand times that he would follow to the letter any orders she gave him. He was not unaware how dear she was to the marquis, and felt he owed her the same deference he would have shown were she Monsieur de Clémengis's sister.

Ernestine accepted his offers of service; she opened her heart to him, expounded on the marquis's kindnesses, on the gratitude she would always feel for them; and entrusting to Monsieur Lefranc's hands her jewels, her precious stones, and several fungible possessions, she instructed him to sell them and have the money transferred to Monsieur de Clémengis, but never to reveal to him its source. Then she entreated him to arrange with Mademoiselle Duménil to borrow against her country estate in order to augment the sum, and beseeched him to act quickly and secretly.

Monsieur Lefranc knew that Ernestine owed her fortune to Monsieur de Clémengis, but he did not know what means he had employed in her favor. Her message had persuaded him that this fortune derived from the marquis, and his first instinct on seeing her so distressed had been to think that, in the present circumstance, she wished to take measures with him concerning her interests.[37]

Surprise mixed with admiration left him speechless for a few moments; he looked at Ernestine, shifted his eyes to the items she was entrusting to him, looked back at her, seeming to doubt whether he had understood. "Do

---

[37]That is, to protect her holdings from the ruin that had befallen the marquis.

you hesitate to do my bidding?" she asked him uneasily. "No, Mademoiselle, no," he said, "I shall fulfill your desires, I shall perhaps surpass them: rest assured I shall faithfully acquit the purpose for which you see fit to employ me. Monsieur le Marquis has well invested his heart's affections; it is my wish that heaven will restore to him the comte de Saint-Servains, his fortune, his health, and preserve for him so tender and respectable a friend as you."

"His health!" Ernestine interrupted impulsively. "Oh God, could he be ill?" "Do not be alarmed, Mademoiselle," replied Monsieur Lefranc, "he was; he was very ill, but is doing better. I hope to see him soon; if things go as I anticipate, I shall be at Clémengis before week's end. Calm yourself, Mademoiselle, I shall not leave without obtaining instructions from you; perhaps I shall write to you what the fear of raising false hopes in your heart prevents me from telling you at this time." As he finished speaking, he bowed respectfully and took his leave of her.

What new bitterness entered Ernestine's soul! The marquis de Clémengis unhappy, the marquis de Clémengis ill, perhaps in danger! How to bear this cruel thought? Though Henriette's silence showed that she disapproved of her action, and though the fear of displeasing this true friend introduced some indecision into her plans, the marquis's condition outweighed every consideration that could still stop her. She wrote to Mademoiselle Duménil.

Henriette was prevailed upon to lend her a chaise[38] and one of her servants to precede her, and to send her post horses, as the letter urged her to do. At noon, Madame de Ranci and Ernestine departed.

What impatience during the trip, what sighs, what tears! "Oh, what if I were never to see him again?" she kept saying to Madame de Ranci. "What if heaven took him from me, if I were condemned to mourn his death! Oh, could I live, and say to myself, and repeat, he is gone?"

A night spent in grieving, so much turmoil and agitation, and the fatigue of the journey exhausted her strength; before the second day was over, she was obliged to stop in a small village: she could not bear the movement of the chaise, and was constantly fainting. Madame de Ranci finally prevailed upon her reason and her friendship to take some nourishment and rest. A long and peaceful sleep refreshed her, and put her in a condition to continue her journey the next day, arriving at Clémengis on the second evening.

Several of the marquis's servants knew Ernestine; the first to spot her ran to announce her arrival to their master. He could not believe them. She entered. He saw her, still doubting it was she. She came forward, trembling, fell to her knees before his bed, took the hand he extended to

---

[38]A light carriage.

her, pressed it feebly in her own, kissed it, and flooded it with her tears.

"Is it she? Is it Ernestine?" the marquis repeated, and he bade her rise and take a seat beside him. "How can it be? My charming friend deigns to come see me! Dear Ernestine! What a sweet, what a lovely surprise! Oh how little I expected this precious favor."

"Now why, Monsieur, why did you not expect it?" she asked, in a most touching voice. "Did you place me among friends whom disgrace estranges? Did you think me insensitive, ungrateful? Have you forgotten that you are everything in creation to me? Oh, if my presence, if my care, if the strongest tokens of my affection can mitigate your sufferings, speak, Monsieur, speak, and I shall never leave you again; every moment of my life will be happy if there is a single one each day when the sight of me, my eagerness to please you, dissipates the recollection of your losses, and brings a ray of joy into your soul."

Monsieur de Clémengis's face turned red all over; he took Ernestine's hands, and flooded them with burning tears. "Oh how," he cried, "did I sacrifice the greatest happiness to vain courtesies, my most ardent desires to bizarre prejudices? Is it Ernestine, is it that amiable girl whom I sacrificed to avid ambition, to mad pride, who preserves for me the tenderest sentiments? She seeks out a man who is fallen, perhaps banished! Her generous compassion attracts her to this wilderness, she comes here to console me: oh, the pains she deigns to share are already diminished; everything else now gives way in my heart to the regret of being unable to return her kindnesses."

Ernestine was about to speak when a jumble of voices made itself heard. The door opened suddenly. Monsieur Lefranc, swept rather than ushered in by the marquis's servants, entered, exclaiming, "Your suit is won unanimously, Monsieur; they are speaking with the comte de Saint-Servains; his accusers are under arrest: I did not want anyone but me to bring you this good news."

"My uncle exonerated, my suit won!" exclaimed the marquis. "Well, then I can follow my heart's inclinations, and reward such love, nobility, and virtues. Come, my dear Ernestine, come," he repeated, transported with pleasure; "come into thy husband's arms. My children," he said to his servants, who were shedding tears of joy, "my dear children, meet your mistress." And extending his hand to Monsieur Lefranc, he said, "And you, my zealous, honest friend: be the first to congratulate the marquise de Clémengis."

Thereupon, cries of delight filled the room. Ernestine was loved, respected; she deserved the happiness she was to enjoy. Madame de Ranci raised her hands to heaven, gave thanks, embraced Ernestine, pronounced tender blessings on the marquis and on her. Monsieur Lefranc, betraying the secret that had been entrusted to him, told Monsieur de Clémengis about Ernestine's generous deed. She alone, still fearing for a life so dear to her, dared not surrender herself to joy. They reassured her; the marquis was weak, but convalescing, and pleasure was about to restore his health . . .

But let us spare the possibly weary reader details more lengthy than interesting. He can easily imagine the happiness of two such tender lovers. The comte de Saint-Servains, avenged of his enemies, resumed the functions of his ministry; he forgave his nephew a marriage that made him happy. Henriette shared in her friend's happiness. Madame de Ranci returned to her retreat, where the attentions of Madame de Clémengis anticipated her desires; and I, who have nothing more to say about this sweet and affectionate Ernestine, shall perhaps busy myself with some other woman's anxieties and troubles.

END